Ray Brown

ENTER AT YOUR OWN RISK

Tales of the Strange and Supernatural

BY RAY BROWN

RoseDog Books
PITTSBURGH, PENNSYLVANIA 15222

ISBN # 0-8059-9560-9
Printed in the United States of America

First Printing

For information or to order additional books, please write:
RoseDog Books
701 Smithfield St.
Pittsburgh, PA 15222
U.S.A.
1-800-834-1803
Or visit our web site and
on-line bookstore at www.rosedogbookstore.com

In Loving Memory of Don Teague, a true friend,
and for my granddaughters, Tiffany and Malena.

DEVOTION TO DUTY

He could feel himself falling. He reached out, hands flailing, grabbing for a banister that was not there, his thick bifocals still on the bureau, and—hell! No wonder he could not see clearly! Then the nighttime steps slammed one by one against him as he somersaulted, screaming, from the landing to the hall tree waiting at the foot of the stairs.

Pain...

Falling again, this time through a darkness that washed around him and spun him into deeper and blacker depths.

Voices.

"Starting the I.V. drip..."

"Don't move him yet."

"Clear his mouth."

He heard himself choking and then saying quite distinctly, "I'm perfectly all right."

But the pain! The waves of darkness!

Ever since that accident, things had not been right. He had trouble remembering. Entire weeks were gone, eradicated from his brain, lost! True, he had been in the hospital and, yes, they had doped him up to ease the pain. That much he did recall. But what of August? How could September have replaced July?

Arthur Marshfield drifted through the twilight before waking. He knew he must rouse himself, scorn the alarm clock's seven AM shriek, be up and out long before the sun rose, for this was no ordinary day. This was September's special day, that once-a-year adrenaline-pumping longed-for moment that made summer endurable. This was the first day of the new school year, and no timepiece had ever dictated when to rise and shine on such a day—not to Arthur Marshfield, not in forty-one Septembers come and gone.

He loved teaching the way others loved their families or even themselves. Colleagues might scoff at his devotion to the tedium of high school English, might ask how he endured the decades of illegible compositions and arrogant youths, but he would simply smile, for he could not offer a logical reply. What would the questioners have said if interrogated about their own particular passions—women, baseball, perhaps even religion? What indeed?

Love was an emotion.

Emotions defied intellectual analysis.

He stirred, aware he must wake up, must start for school. His classroom must be set to rights, desktops scrubbed if the custodians had been lazy, course outlines prepared, chalkboards written on, roll books organized, seating charts constructed, the week's lessons perfected. He was always the first person to arrive at school, every day, year in and year out, and today must be no exception.

He had set a record of sorts. Not once in forty-one years had he ever taken a sick day. Even that accident on the stairs had failed to blemish his perfect attendance record, for it had occurred in late July, summer vacation. Never out sick. Not once. He was damned proud of that.

He opened his eyes.

Still dark. Plenty of time yet.

Then a doubt. Was this actually the first day of school?

He stared into the blackness above him, his limbs rigid, a burning spot of panic deep at the base of his skull, a spot that spread even as he lay there. What day was this? *What day was this?* He did not know. He could not remember a calendar date, nor bring to mind yesterday either—what he had done, where he had gone, anything at all. And what of the principal's customary letter—oh, a formality that served little purpose, that annual Xeroxed paper mailed to each teacher a week before school's re-opening ("Dear Faculty Member:

I trust your summer was both restful and rewarding, and that you anticipate the upcoming academic year with renewed fervor. We have made several changes in our faculty since last June, et cetera, et cetera.")—yes, what of that letter? Had he received one this year?

Lost! Moments, hours, days! Come and gone and he like a video camera suddenly shut off during it all, his playback incomplete!

That accursed accident!

It had infested his brain cells with amnesia!

Arthur Marshfield began to feel cold, terribly cold. How would he teach if this continued? He would be unable to recollect the names of his students—or what he was supposed to cover on a given day—or what he had already covered.

He groaned in anguish.

But forty-one years! He must not let forty-one years slip away because of an accident. For he was obsessed with his job, always had been, always would be. It was his sole purpose for existence, his very heartbeat!

He would not give it up. Nothing could make him do that. Not now. Not ever.

No letter from the principal was needed. *Instinct* announced that this was the first day of classes.

Arthur Marshfield struggled up.

But it was a long walk to the high school. Far longer than when he had lived three blocks away.

Tardy for the first time in his scholastic career, he reached the door to his classroom. A group of students lurched out of their seats. A teacher he had never met shrieked.

He opened his mouth to speak, to demand the identity of this usurper...

But little more than a rush of air hissed from his throat. His vocal cords would not function.

Arthur Marshfield tottered into the classroom, trailing the rank odor of graveyard dirt behind him.

EYE FOR AN EYE

That October in 1937 I stood before an empty grave while a terrible chill seeped from the soil and entwined my legs like an icy ectoplasm. I was eleven years old but what filled my head were thoughts no child that age should have. My slamming heart gradually slowed; my breathing returned to normal. On the ground a shovel glinted.

Cold silver light shimmered from between the rows of tree trunks. How late it must be! Grandma would be angry if I were late for supper.

Before I was halfway to the farmhouse, gray sky had changed to black and the dirt road had become the dark side of the moon, soil imploding into unseen craters. I shivered in rhythm to my thudding shoes and fumbled with the buttons on my denim jacket. By the time our house came into view, my thick blond hair was glued to my forehead and I was wheezing like an old man.

"Hi, Grandma," I gasped, bursting into the kitchen.

With a shrill screech of scraping wood, she shoved back her chair. "Where were you, Bobby?"

I studied my shoes. "Playing. That's all. Playing."

"You're caked with sweat–and dirt!"

I kept my gaze directed downward. Some portion of my mind noticed that the shoelaces were frayed, the shoes scuffed and shabby. I also sensed my sister's smug delight, and–suspecting betrayal–wanted to punch her.

"Jennifer says you played hooky from school. Is that true, young man?"

"Uh huh." I raised my head. From her chair eight-year-old Jennifer stuck out her tongue, then swallowed a mouthful of spaghetti without chewing. With that mop of red curls and saucer eyes she looked like a real-life version of Little Orphan Annie, the kid in the Harold Gray comic strip our small town's newspaper had finally begun to carry. Jennifer could double for Annie, except that Annie had a faithful dog named Sandy and my sister did not. At the moment I wished Sandy would appear and take a big bite out of Jennifer's behind.

"This is the third time this week! I thought you liked school."

I squirmed uncomfortably.

"Why did you skip classes?"

I remained mute.

"Why, Bobby?"

"You wouldn't understand."

Countenance white as her hair, the old woman swayed and her mouth quivered while her faded eyes searched for an answer in my defiant ones. "Oh God, Bobby, I know it hasn't been easy for you since your mama went away, but Jennifer has had to contend with the same thing, and she doesn't skip school!"

"No." But Jennifer had not seen what I had...

"Why do you do it, Bobby? Why do you bring me such heartache? Your mama is my little girl, and whenever she runs off I come close to dying. Now you set about disgracing me too. Why, child? Haven't I been good to you?"

I nodded, ashamed. I did not want to hurt my grandmother.

"Go upstairs to your room."

Pity almost overcame my determination. "Grandma, I had a reason for what I did. A good reason."

She waited, but I clamped my lips together and forced back the confession. Jennifer was beaming. Stupid little kid! Just because I bullied her sometimes, she wanted to see me get a beating. Okay, Jennifer, enjoy what happens! But I'm doing this for you and Grandma as well as me...

"I'll be up shortly," declared Grandma, and added, more for herself than me, "Maybe if I'd punished your mama when she was a little girl she wouldn't be the way she is today. The idea! The very idea! Running off and abandoning the two of you at the drop of a hat!"

Tears already trickling, I trudged up the steps to my room and huddled on the bed. I loved that wretched old woman who had endured more than anyone should, and the last thing I desired was to create more sorrow. Grandma never used a belt and her frail hands were incapable of inflicting much damage, so the punishment would be a humiliation, nothing more. My tears were for her—for the new pain she suffered, all because of me.

If only I could tell her...

"An eye for an eye, a tooth for a tooth." Hammurabi's Code. Laws originated by a pagan king of Babylon almost two thousand years before the birth of Christ. How often Dad had said that today's world would be better off if governments followed that ancient code of retribution! And it made sense when you considered it carefully. If a killer strangled someone, shouldn't that killer in turn be strangled? Jail wasn't the answer, but a lot of murderers went to jail or even got off completely because of "intimidated juries and slick lawyers," as Dad had been fond of saying. The killer's victim cried out for revenge. An eye for an eye...

From the bedroom walls elaborate crayon portraits of Dracula and Frankenstein snarled, but all I saw was my father, a man with long limbs and cadaverous complexion, myopia making him a zombie unless you knew the man and loved him as I had. Kind, tranquil, patient, Dad had devoted himself to farming and to historical academia—a bizarre blending of practicality and scholarship. My most potent memory of the man? Dad, exhausted from a hard day's labor, lanky body stretched on the sofa, H.G. Wells' History of the World open on his lap.

"Wish you were here," I thought.

But Dad had died three years ago. The stroke had been instantaneous.

And now, twelfth birthday next month, I was the man of the family, although Grandma still treated me as a baby. Dad dead, Mama gone too...

Grandma entered with obvious reluctance. "You've got talent," she said. "Look at those drawings—and the papier-mâché dragons! You could sell your art, and you're only in sixth grade. You always talk about going to art school when you're older. Keep on the way you are and all the talent in the world won't help you."

Moments later, as I bent over the mattress and writhed under a surprisingly powerful crescendo of thwacks, I spoiled it for my sister by not hollering.

Around nine o'clock, just as I nudged sleep, Grandma sat on the edge of the bed and stroked my forehead. "Bobby, I'm sorry I punished you."

"It's okay, Grandma. Honest."

"It's not okay! But your shenanigans drive me crazy. First your mama takes to running off, and then you behave like rules don't mean a thing. I'm out of my mind with worry!"

There was nothing to say.

She sighed. "I keep praying your mama will get some sense into that thick skull of hers and settle down, but she was always stubborn." She gripped my hand. "You scare me, child. You're as willful as your mama. You have secrets, things you won't talk about..."

I didn't move, didn't breathe, felt bugs of perspiration creep along my stomach. Did she suspect?

"Please, Bobby, try to behave at school. I can't take much more strain."

I sucked in the cool October air. No, she hadn't guessed...

Grandma kissed me. "Get a good sleep, Bobby."

* * * * *

The sleep was far from good. For hours memories churned. Dad piggy-backed me into the parlor while I, chortling as only a four-year-old can, shot him with a toy pistol. "You got me!" Dad shouted. "Any more holes and I'll look like Swiss cheese!"

"You shouldn't let him play with guns," Mama said. "Not even toy ones."

And I was speaking, demanding, "I wanna shoot things! Teach me how to shoot!"

"When you're older," Dad said. "Then you can use my revolver. Only on tin cans, though."

Other scenes kaleidoscoped as I moaned and twisted.

Dad, showing me how to load the revolver...

Dad again, bushel basket of apples in his hands, smile half-formed, a puzzled question, "What's that funny noise?"

"I don't hear anything, Dad."

My father frowning, "Or is it in my head?"—and another voice, my own, shrieking while Dad fell, apples careening as the basket, too, toppled...

And Mama, youthful at thirty-four. "You can't expect me to mourn your father for the rest of my life. Please, please, try to understand!"

I had tried, in imagination conjuring a new father who looked and sounded and somehow was my real one.

Months of newcomers to the house, men who smiled too much and brought toys, men who in no way resembled Dad, men I hated, usurpers...

And Mama, different, no longer preoccupied with her children, concerned instead with unannounced trips, nocturnal disappearances, spur-of-the-moment telephone calls to Grandma, "Can you stay with the kids again? No, I don't know how long. I can't stand being here in this house, I've got to get away, I'm suffocating!" Soon Grandma had become a permanent resident in our home, a stand-in parent who aged more and more as Mama vanished for weeks at a time. Mama, whose temper fluctuated erratically...

Part of the problem, of course, was money. Dad had put some aside for emergencies, and Grandma had her own savings, but the tiny farm had never been especially profitable. With Dad out of the picture, all of us struggled to eke out an existence, but Jennifer and I were kids and there was, after all, a limit to how much we two could do to make crops grow and still attend school. Mama seldom spoke of money problems in front of us, but we guessed that these were at least partially responsible for her moodiness and irascibility.

Of course there was Dad's death itself.

"When they buried him, they buried a part of her, too, " Grandma often murmured. "It takes time. She'll be herself again."

Then, last year, two men began to visit on a weekly basis, albeit different nights. Jack Gillon and Arthur Hershoff. Both lived within walking distance, both were in their early forties, and neither looked or acted like my father.

"Which one do you like better?" Mama sometimes asked. "Jack or Arthur?"

Jennifer always giggled and said she couldn't make up her mind; I said nothing.

And there were nights when I could not fall asleep, for sounds would reach my bedroom from Mama's.

Jack Gillon.

Arthur Hershoff.

Sometimes the utterances were soft, crooning.

Other nights, the same voices rose in anger, for Mama's moods were unpredictable and alcohol made things worse. Mama, shouting, shouting...

And a voice, Grandma's, cautionary. "What you do is immoral! Worse, dangerous! These men you parade into your bedroom night after night—do they know about each other? You're begging for disaster!"

Now, struggling against these night visions, I fought my way to total wakefulness and, mortified, discovered Jennifer gaping at my wet face.

"You were crying," she said. "I got up to get a glass of water. You okay?"

I wiped my eyes. "Yeah. Bad dreams, that's all. Go back to bed before you wake up Grandma."

She left, a fluttering ghost in her white nightgown. And a realization sunk in: she had not come to gloat or ridicule. She had come because she cared about me.

I rested my forehead against the cool wood of the footboard. "I don't want to be mean to you, Jennifer," I thought. "But I hurt. I miss Mama so much, and I need to take it out on someone. Maybe you feel the same way. Maybe that's why you do things to me."

But soon, very soon, all the hatred and rage would burst forth in one carefully planned act and I would be free of all that was stoppered up inside. An eye for an eye...

Jack Gillon's eyes were ice blue—the kind that hid passion...

Arthur Hershoff's eyes? Always bloodshot. Too much whiskey, too little sleep. Did Hershoff worry? Toss and turn in his bed?

Eyes...

I squeezed mine shut. But one scene replayed a million times. One night weeks ago I had drifted through a restless sleep in which furious voices raged. Then, a full-mooned sky, a silhouetted man staggering beneath his burden, so far away that face and figure were unrecognizable.

What had awakened me that night long gone? A sudden premonition? All I recalled was my bedroom window, the bleak landscape, and that man who had no automobile.

That man who carried something into the woods...

In the morning, Mama was gone. So were her suitcase and some of her clothes. Grandma had sighed in resignation. "Your mama will be back in a few days," she told us, for Mama had run off without a word six times in the last year.

"She's man crazy," Jennifer pronounced, quoting what we had both overheard Grandma muttering upon occasion. I squeezed my sister's shoulder hard. "You don't even know what that means, so shut up!"

"She'll be back in a few days," Grandma reiterated. But days stretched into weeks and Mama never returned.

"Head over heels for some man," Grandma told us, finally.

"She's gone because of a man?" Jennifer asked, sounding betrayed.

"Afraid so, honey," said Grandma.

I agreed. Mama was gone because of a man. But a man who lived close, a man on foot, not some stranger she had met in a bar. Jack Gillon? Arthur Hershoff? One or the other, in all probability.

Which one?

"Call the sheriff," I thought, and discarded the notion. It was all speculation. I had no proof.

Only the memory of a drunken fracas, quick and vehement, penetrating the wall of my bedchamber, over so soon that Grandma at the other end of the house and my slugabed sister heard nothing; abrupt silence; and, later, a man outdoors, carrying something into the woods...

* * * * *

Halloween was lurking in its costumed shadows, five days hence. Preparations were underway. Grandma had purchased apples and was concocting homemade taffy, though few children ever ventured so far from the main streets of the nearby town. Pumpkins sat in the downstairs windows, faces ready for an orange fever. Crayoned goblins grimaced from huge sheets of newsprint thumbtacked to the front door. Jennifer spent hours in Grandma's room, rooting through trunks of antiquated clothes in quest of the perfect costume.

And I also prepared. Time and again I disappeared on foot into the woods and to the grave, satisfying myself that nothing had been disturbed. Other days at the close of school I hurried the mile and a half home, arriving long before my dawdling sister, so that I would have an hour or so to work on my secret project before I had to do chores. In the attic I labored with paste, torn newspaper, coat hangers, and eventually paint.

"Why can't I go up there?" Jennifer complained each evening at the supper table. "Why do you have the key to the attic and I don't?"

"It's a surprise. A Halloween surprise! Wait and see."

And Grandma would wink at me conspiratorially, for in order to get the key I had been obliged to confess my scheme. With papier-mâché, old clothes, and my indisputable artistic talent, I was constructing a monster. "I'm going to tie a lot of coat-hanger wire together for its framework," I had told Grandma. "I'll wrap rags around the wire to pad its arms and legs and body. I'll put clothes on it, and use papier-mâché to make the face and hands. Can I use that old wheelchair? You know, to put it in and take it trick-or-treating?"

The wheelchair, currently collecting dust in the attic, had belonged to some long-ago relative.

"All right," said Grandma, no doubt recollecting some of the more malicious pranks she had played as a child on Halloween. "You don't plan to soap store windows, do you?"

"No. I just want to take the monster with me."

"All right," she said again.

* * * * *

Halloween. Six p.m.

Jennifer and Grandma waited breathlessly while I went to fetch my surprise. “Hurry, hurry!” Gypsy Jennifer shouted. “Sally Ann’s mother will be here any second to take me trick-or-treating.”

After much thumping and thudding to get everything down the attic stairs, I returned.

In spite of herself, Grandma gasped. Seated in the wheelchair, legs and arms stiff in feigned death, body crusted with dry mud, a horror approached.

“Oh, it’s wonderful!” squealed Jennifer. “Look at the hands—all shriveled and twisted, almost like a skeleton.”

Pride momentarily stifled my fears. “Does it look real?”

“Too real!” said Grandma. She edged closer. Not until she touched the hands did she relax. Only papier-mâché. But she’d had her doubts. That was obvious.

“Oh, I wish I could come with you,” said Jennifer. “I’d love to see people’s faces when you bring that up to their front porches. But I told Sally Ann I’d go with her.”

“You’ll get a lot more goodies than I will,” I reminded her. “Sally Ann’s mother is going to drive you to town. You’ll get to go to a lot of different houses. All I’m going to do is visit a few of the people around here.”

“Don’t worry,” said Grandma. “I’ll have plenty of taffy left. I made much too much.”

We separated, Grandma to present treats to those few witches and goblins brave enough to materialize this far from the main roads, Jennifer to await her ride, I to transport my monster.

* * * * *

The first three stops were uneventful. Old Mrs. O’Hara shook her head, muttering about sick minds, but produced a tasty cupcake. At the Tolliver home little Mark, age three, screamed in fright, but despite the child’s hysteria I received both candy and delighted compliments from Mark’s father. The Bartholomews had to examine the monster for five minutes, with small giggles and uncertain fingers, before they would contribute to my trick-or-treat bag.

The fourth stop was at Arthur Hershoff's home on a dark side road. I paused to remove the mask covering my creation's true face before approaching the porch. Leaving the wheelchair and its rider out of sight at the side of the house and climbing the wooden steps, I stood immobile on that sagging porch, a terrible coldness in the pit of my stomach. "Can't do this," I thought. But I rang the bell.

"Yeah?" Arthur Hershoff was in the doorway, tall and muscular, those bloodshot eyes glinting. Then he recognized his visitor. "Hello, Bobby! Here for treats? Wait a second."

Though filled with invisible chalk dust, my mouth somehow worked. "I want to show you something."

Hershoff was interested. "Oh yeah? What?"

"Over here. I found it..."

Together we walked into the gloom.

The man stared in perplexion. "I knew you were talented," he said, at last. "You made this, I bet. Halloween ghoul, huh? Pretty realistic. But–" (He peered uncertainly at the wheelchair's occupant) "–why did you make it look like that?"

I had scrutinized his reaction and was anxious to leave.

"Don't forget your candy," Hershoff called. "Here. Some for your sister too. Say, when's your mother coming back?"

"I can't say, Mr. Hershoff."

* * * * *

Last stop. Jack Gillon's, an isolated cabin near the woods. Through undraped windows he was visible adjusting his radio.

"I've got something to show you," I said. My legs threatened to buckle and my lips twitched. Gillon did not notice and followed me outdoors to the rear of the cabin.

"You didn't think I'd find her, did you?" I asked, as the wheelchair came into view. Though my hand was already inside the trick-or-treat bag, my gaze was on Gillon, judging.

The man's mouth fell open. A sobbing scream began deep within his chest.

From the wheelchair, a muddy corpse glared, decomposing face still suggestive, blond hair intact.

I shot Jack Gillon, the explosion thunderous in the October silence.

Then, sick to my stomach, I collapsed on the ground and waited. But no one came.

* * * * *

Half an hour later, I had managed to push the wheelchair some distance along little used dirt paths in the woods. I had been unobserved. Not that it mattered. Witnesses had already seen the papier-mâché monster.

Gillon was much heavier than the monster, so I leaned panting against a tree. "Hurry!" I thought. "Before Grandma gets worried about you!"

I cleared away the branches, leaves, and rubbish that concealed the grave I had dug. With desperate determination I rolled Jack Gillon into that grave. The man lay on his back, monster mask still over his face, mud-caked winding sheet hiding the rags and bandages that sealed the hole in his heart and prevented a bloody trail. Grimacing, I removed the monster mask, for I must put it back on my creation.

From the underbrush I retrieved my shovel and buried the man, dragged dry leaves over the mound, tossed the shovel deep into the woods, and wearily started the return trek to Gillon's cabin. The papier-mâché figure was there, waiting...

Overhead, the black sky crackled with light. A raindrop pelted my nose. Good! Better than planned! Rain would quickly blend new-turned earth with old, would wash away evidence. Our town was indeed small and we boasted but a single law enforcement official, a doddering sheriff in his eighties, so the odds were with me. Yet the rain was a godsend, and my terror abated somewhat.

I staggered through the rain, while ahead of me the wheelchair bounced. "They won't arrest me," I panted, repeating the sentence until it became a mantra. "They won't even guess he's dead." And why should anyone think otherwise? The man lived alone. For his own particular reasons he leaves for good. End of story.

But he's dead, dead, dead, dead! sang the tires of the wheelchair. *They'll find out, out, out, out!*

Who would find out? The ancient sheriff? Not likely. He never even figured out that your mother was murdered. No one did. Except you.

"Mama," I sobbed.

If only I knew where she was buried...

Her name was on no headstone.

But neither was her killer's

An eye for an eye!

VIGIL

Nicky's eyes were the color of moonlight; his sleek fur a part of the black sky. He was a shadow amongst shadows, there atop the cinderblock wall that crowded against the pines.

Somewhere a dog barked.

Headlights swung into the parking lot.

Teenage voices rose and fell.

Nicky remained motionless. He was a shadow and understood that he must not move...not yet...

The voices grew nearer.

Nicky waited. He did not know the name of the one he wanted, but he was aware of the young man's scent. A month ago, a week ago, even yesterday Nicky would never have been capable of such patience. Tonight all was different. *He* was different...

Yesterday Nicky had liked people, trusted them. Had, after a fashion, *loved* Mark, the young schoolteacher who provided food and water and murmurs of kindness. But that had been yesterday. Now, tonight, this very moment, Nicky missed Mark—but loved no one, had lost that ability.

Wind hissed through the pines, a cat's cry of fear and rage. The voices were much closer now, one scent stronger than all the rest. Nicky did not move. Mark's image flickered, but Mark was not the one he awaited; Mark was not part of the approaching voices.

The shadow crouched on top of the wall lost its purpose for an instant. Nicky drifted, as he often had while sleeping, toward the past. Memories stirred themselves. Nicky was suddenly the size of a man's fist and mewing for his mother. Then, somewhat larger, he was picking himself up from the side of the road as a huge shiny thing sped away on spinning feet. Hunger...loneliness...and terror. He was more afraid than something his size could possibly be. How could he contain so much panic? He was bloated with the emotion—bursting with it—and out it came, spewing forth in one long unending and agonized scream...

Giants, then...people...and he, rumbling with joy, carried from what they called "parknnnlah" to a place of unnatural coolness and delicious smells. He was petted, fussed over—more importantly, fed.

They made funny noises, explosive guffaws of sound, when he lapped at spilled foam on the tavern's floor. "Boozy," they named him, and the name stuck during the four days he was there.

On the fifth Mark appeared, taller than most of them, his voice softer. He ate at one of the tables in the chill gloom. When Nicky brushed against his trousers, Mark had bent down and scooped him up.

Words were exchanged between Mark and the others, and later Nicky curled on Mark's lap as another of the huge shiny things with spinning feet carried them somewhere.

"Boozy," Mark muttered. "Terrible name. Let's call you something else."

Nicky purred at the unintelligible sounds.

"Let me see..." A pause. "You were living in that restaurant, The Nickelodeon. How about calling you Nickelodeon? Yeah. That's okay! Nickelodeon. Nicky, for short."

For short...for short ...for short... Nicky floated on the waves of words, unable to comprehend them, aware of their warmth, their pulsebeat, and their safety. His mother's heart thrummed its song, safe, safe, safe, safe...

The raucous sounds killed his lovebeat. Nicky was on the wall again and the one he wanted was much nearer now, so close his scent was a stench of sweat and cigarettes and beer. Even yesterday Nicky's senses had failed to perceive so clearly—but tonight was a new world.

Black clouds scudded across the moon, murdering what little light there was.

The stench enveloped Nicky as the teenagers weaved drunkenly toward the wall. Wind shrieked through tree limbs, warning them away. And the moon blinked from beneath the clouds, an angry yellow eye, feline, inhuman, cold...

Cold...

Nicky lost his focus. Cold. Cold. Where was he? Gray metal walls, the air like ice, empty bottle pressing into his back, wet newspapers covering his mouth, decaying food fouling each breath with a reek almost visible, green and thick and heavy. Human noises, too...laughter of the vilest sort...a face, invisible because of the scrap of newspaper obscuring Nicky's eyes, but sensed nevertheless...a face watching from the top of the gray metal walls, a face that gloated and grinned as the coldness intensified and all laughter and sounds ebbed...

Cold...

Nicky darted to another moment of cold, a *safer* moment, far *safer*...

Locked outdoors, a November eve, Mark asleep within the mobile home. Scratch the screen door, call to him, screech about the change in weather—all to no avail. Mark, cut off by heavy winter glass behind the mesh of summer screens. Scratch some more, yowl like an infant, but unaware of it all Mark sleeps. Warm at ten PM, then the chilling breath, winter come too soon and unannounced, and Mark cannot be roused.

Cold. Too cold.

Mark's toy—that thing he plays with in the tiny back yard—lawnmower, lawnmower—leaning against the side of the mobile home, handles against the ventilator grate...

Clamber up it, that's the way, and leap...

And Mark awakens with a shriek. Weight on his chest, as darkness leaps from the dark.

"Nicky! You scared the hell outa me! How'd you get in here?"

Through the loose ventilator grid...squeezing past the water heater...clawing open a poorly tacked veneer panel that opens under the bathroom sink. Then the joyous leap onto the bed...onto Mark.

But Mark fails to guess. "Jesus, cat, I locked you outdoors for the night. You're a damn Houdini! I mean it. Never heard of any cat that could break into a locked house! You're kinda incredible, Nicky. Kinda frightening, too."

He strokes, pets, all the while continuing the outpour of words that mean little to an animal but confirm that safety and happiness are real.

Ripples of rumbling...waves of it, waves and waves of purring...a tide that sweeps from then to now...

Now.

Now!

The shadow on the wall was back, washed up from the tide pool of memory, and the night was as cold as that gray dumpster had been, and the one Nicky wanted walked beneath him, walked oblivious to the patch of night that crouched above. Two other young men accompanied the one who reeked of sweat and cigarettes and beer, but they were as unreal to Nicky as forgotten dreams.

Now!

The shadow moved at last, detaching itself from the rest of the night, lunging off the wall and into the air. The wind howled Nicky's rage—and need.

The young man sensed his danger, jerked his eyes up, and half raised an arm to ward off the unseen.

But nothing was there.

Nothing except a patch of darkness floating against a landscape of other darknesses. As the young man gaped in disbelief, the drifting shadow—which was no larger than an alley cat—fell silently over his head, his face.

And, for one brief instant, the young man knew how Nicky had felt after the young man had left him there in that dumpster.

"Whazza matter?" one of his intoxicated buddies demanded. "You look funny!"

He did look funny. His skin had purpled in the moonlight, veins bulged in his neck and temples, while his eyes seemed to swell as though a hangman's noose had snapped taut. For a heartbeat he swayed.

Then all was as it had been. He looked normal once more.

But when his companions asked him what had happened, he shoved them away and wandered off into the night. Not long ago he had enjoyed getting so soused that patting a friendly cat had been a mere prelude to picking it up and drop-kicking it, then depositing the broken-backed thing in a trash bin. Now, tonight, he was different.

He set out to explore the world from this new vantage point, this new height, on two legs instead of four.

He hummed to himself. A casual wayfarer would have sworn the young man was purring.

THE WITCH

Halloween night. A yellow splotch of moon hung in the sky, peeking from churning clouds. Red and orange leaves slithered across sidewalks and people's front lawns. The wind hissed a warning.

It was late, nearly midnight. All the trick-or-treaters had long since vanished. Streets were silent, save for wind or an occasional car. This small town in upstate New York locked its doors, drew its curtains, on another October 31.

But Billy Purvis was still up and about. Oh yes. Billy Purvis, age twelve, who peered from beneath his ghoul mask at the mist-shrouded street lamps and the silent, dead avenues. Billy Purvis wasn't ready to close the coffin lid on another Halloween. Not Billy! There were still things to be done, evils to be worked, and Billy was just the boy to do them.

He was tall for his age. Broad-shouldered, too. Beneath the false face his own features hid, strong even features that suggested a bovine placidity. His eyes gave him away. They were tiny and mean, the eyes of a snake—or a bully.

Billy Purvis delighted in his size and strength. Countless schoolmates had groveled at his feet. He was afraid of no one, or so he told himself.

No one except the witch.

The witch lived behind wrought-iron gates on top of the hill that overlooked St. Mary's Cemetery. The witch was wealthy. The witch owned a ramshackle old mansion of decayed wood, crumbling porticos, boarded-up windows. But there were crystal chandeliers in that mansion, and (according to Billy's old man one time when he was sober) marble fireplaces, fancy French oil paintings, and museum-quality statues.

Billy Purvis, who came from a poor family, had always hated the witch. Other people—grown-ups—called her "Mrs. Tyler" or "Harriet"... but he knew who she was ...what she was...

Harriet Tyler. Forever ancient. Hair as fine as spider-webs, skin wrinkled and pale, eyes that could see in the dark—he was sure they could!

Harriet Tyler, with lumpy shapeless dresses, old lady shoes with a multitude of laces, and always, always a black cat for company. *Witch!*

He shivered as a sudden gust of wind whipped beneath his unbuttoned topcoat. He had swiped that coat from the hall closet at home while the old man was in the kitchen pouring another shot of gin. What a perfect disguise! Who would ever guess a kid was here, this night, acting as an avenger? Tall dude in a monster mask and drab outdated topcoat that dragged in the dirt? It couldn't be little Billy Purvis! Certainly not! Little Billy was only a child.

Avenger, he thought, and grinned, a nasty vicious grin. *Yeah, that's the ticket. I'm an avenger.*

He was exactly that. Already tonight he had invaded numerous properties, slinking from the shadows to sink his feet into jack o' lanterns that had offered candle-shine welcomes.

How many pumpkins on front porches had he smashed? Ten? At least that! Maybe twelve or thirteen. There were plenty of kids at school he hated. Plenty who deserved to have their pumpkins kicked apart.

But the best revenge was yet to come. Billy's grin grew more intense, more fierce. Old Harriet Tyler. Got to kill another of her cats. Another of her familiars.

Oh yes, he knew all about familiars. More than a year ago he had seen a TV special about witches. Familiars were demons that helped witches. They came right from the bowels of hell and they always took the shape of something familiar...like a black cat.

Over the past year Billy had scaled that wrought-iron fence surrounding Mrs. Tyler's property at least once a month—and, under the cover of darkness, had sometimes been able to lure the latest cat into destruction with soft words and a fresh can of tuna.

"There's no such thing as witches," the kids at school would say. But Billy knew better. Harriet Tyler was a witch. Even as a very young child, he had sensed it. And if he were wrong about this, so what? She lived in a bigger house than he did and, according to the old man, had so much loot it was squirting out her ears, even if she was too weird to fix up her mansion. So, witch or not, she deserved whatever evil he could do her.

Billy had decapitated the last cat and left its head in her mailbox. This night, All Hallows Eve, he intended a worse fate for her new familiar. He would skin it alive with his buck knife.

He stood panting in front of old Mrs. Tyler's wrought-iron fence. Wind shrieked through the trees. Clouds obscured the moon. To calm himself he took several deep breaths, grabbed the fence, and hauled himself up.

Once inside, he crouched low, sprinting toward the long enclosed porch that sprawled drunkenly from the front to the sides of the house. He halted a few feet from the porch steps. Reached inside his coat pockets. Withdrew a buck knife and a plastic bag loaded with ripe fish. He opened the bag.

"Here, kitty, kitty. Nice kitty..."

Tree branches rattled. The night grew murkier.

"Kitty, kitty, kitty..."

No cat emerged from the gloom. Billy Purvis tried again. "Kitty, kitty, kitty..."

But no cat responded. Mrs. Tyler had not acquired another cat.

Inexplicably, he was afraid. *Forget the whole thing,* he thought. *Just get out of here, okay, man. Okay?*

Then he saw the pumpkin near the foot of the porch steps, its eyes and mouth ablaze with orange light, and he let instinct take over, all fear banished with his first jolting step forward. Even as he grabbed for the hugely-grinning jack-o'-lantern, all set to drop-kick it to hell, he wondered why he had not noticed it earlier...

A split-second later he thought about familiars—demons that were supposed to take physical form to assist witches...

With a roar of goblin joy, the pumpkin seized his hands in its fanged maw—and bit them off.

FLASHBACK

They walked and smiled and said little. All along the concrete path, rainbow-garbed throngs shouted, shoved, guffawed, while vendors hawked their wares: leather goods, hand-painted tee shirts, cheap watches, crayoned caricatures, sunglasses, oil paintings, erotic posters. Sun glittered off the sand and the discarded beer bottles. Wind twisted through the crowds, as did half-naked roller-skaters. A teenage girl whose bikini pants were startlingly like a man's jock strap veered her bike to avoid a huge black man who wore a pink safari hat and silver mummy wrappings.

Venice Beach, California. A Saturday morning on this, the first day of spring. Yellow heat made it unseasonably warm. And everybody in the world was here, reeking of beer and pot and Coppertone, eyes sheathed in polarizing plastic, bodies lathered with sweat and lotion, gooseflesh appearing in the sudden rush of ocean wind, then disappearing like Claude Rains as the breezes died. A dozen portable CD players shrieked warring tunes.

Jason smiled at the young woman whose hand he held. "Want to get out of this mob? Maybe take off our shoes and wade in the surf?"

"Sure," she said. But instead they pushed on through the living obstacle course, careful to dodge skateboarders, eyes sweeping the infinity of vendors and booths.

Cameras for sale–and plastic dog poop–towels, beads, blankets, toys, sunglasses, skull rings with fake-ruby eyes, grotesque earrings that looked like clothespins...

Jason tightened his grip on the young woman's hand. "Wait," he murmured. "I want to look at something." He guided her toward a canvas enclosure, a kind of three-fold screen staked in place by tall posts. Despite the garish red-orange-purple blouses on display, the obviously overpriced and inferior merchandise, the oppressive heat that seemed trapped within the tent-like area—despite these things, Jason moved with determination, easing past overcrowded tables of scarves, books, trinkets, dragging his companion through the press of clothing racks and overweight women.

In front of a tee shirt display he stopped. Powerpuff Girls leered at him from some of the shirts; Zodiac figures and outdated Darth Vaders from others. His gaze was not on these shirts, however. Instead he stood fixated in front of the object above the tee shirt display: a poster among a host of other posters, all strung from a clothesline stretched from one of the enclosure's posts to another.

"What's wrong?" the young woman asked, seeing the expression on his face.

"Nothing." But his eyes never shifted away from the poster.

Puzzled and a little irritated, she examined it. A simple sketch of a hot air balloon, drawn in the simplistic manner of a small child, and below it the caption, "Flying high!"

"Jason?" she said.

He made no reply.

"Jason?"

He continued to stare at the poster. "Looks like a kid drew it," he said, finally.

"Yes?" She made it a question.

"I used to draw pictures like that. You know, when I was maybe five or six."

"I drew things too. So what?" The heat was getting to her.

"It reminds me of something I haven't thought about in years."

"What? Drawing stuff when you were little?"

"No. A parade...must've been in first grade, maybe. It was around Thanksgiving and the Chamber of Commerce sponsored a big parade. Bands and floats and balloons. Not balloons like on that poster. These balloons looked like storybook characters, fairy tale stuff—you know, dragons, Donald Duck, that sort of thing."

He hesitated, eyes on the poster. "My favorite was a gigantic caterpillar. I'd never seen anything like it. Took up the whole city block it was so long—and it was made up of a lot of huge round helium balloons, like so many beads of a necklace strung together. Each part of the caterpillar had black cloth hanging down from it—to help hide the guy who had to hold the balloon's ropes and act as a set of the caterpillar's legs. And the caterpillar was gigantic. Damned monster seemed to stretch out forever! And all those people holding it down and making it bob along in time to the parade music..."

She was clearly impatient. Why babble on about some stupid event that had occurred in some dreary little town in New York State? New York was snow and sleet and freeze-your-ass winters, humid nasty boring summers, dull-witted smugness and self-satisfied complacency—oh, perhaps not in the Big Apple itself, but in the little town he was from? You better believe it! California, in contrast, was gorgeous climate most of the year, an exciting multitude of ethnic groups, a land of freeways to rush you to continual escapes—to Magic Mountain, Disneyland, Universal Studios, beaches, Renaissance Fairs, Knott's Berry Farm, the Hollywood Bowl! You were never bored in California; you were always on the go...

"That caterpillar had the weirdest face—big green head, bulging yellow eyeballs, mouth with a whole bunch of white fangs. I loved that face. Like something out of a comic book, you know? Funny thing, though. Before the parade—two, three days before—they had that same caterpillar all stretched out on the ground at Riverview Field. That was the park a block from where I lived. They hadn't inflated it yet and nobody was guarding it or anything. I remember that my mother and I were coming back from Main Street—I dunno, we'd been shopping at Newberry's, maybe—and as we walked past the park, there it was, that caterpillar. I told my mom that we should go home and come back with scissors so I could cut a big hole in its head. Pretty weird, huh? But little kids have pretty weird ideas sometimes. Guess I thought it would be hysterically funny, a real joke. But Mom said if I did that, how would I get to see the caterpillar in the parade. A real diplomat, my mother!"

He shrugged and glanced at his companion. "I'm rambling. Sorry. But—well, it's this poster. The balloon on it. Somehow it brought the whole thing back to me after all this time. Haven't thought about that parade in years." His gaze shot back to the poster. Then, almost sheepishly: "It does look a lot like the sort of drawings I made when I was little. God! The more I look at it..."

"Come on, Jason, I want to get something to eat."

Still he stared. "I think maybe I *did* draw a balloon like that once—a long time ago." His voice lost volume. "I'd swear I drew a picture exactly like that...*exactly*."

She made a derisive sound.

"I'd swear that's *my* drawing," he muttered, more emphatic than ever.

"Don't be stupid! It's not your drawing. That's impossible!"

But he had at last noticed the tee shirt display. And, like a man greeting an old friend, Jason beamed with real pleasure. "Look at this! I haven't seen one of these since I was a kid."

"It's nothing but a blue tee shirt," she declared. "No big deal. You're acting strange, Jason—and I don't like it."

He held the shirt in one hand, almost caressing the emblem with the other. "Superman," he said. "My favorite TV show when I was growing up. And I owned a shirt exactly like this one."

"Jeez, Jason, plenty of stores sell Superman tee shirts. What do you mean, you haven't seen one since you were a kid? With all those Christopher Reeve movies on DVD and television series like 'Smallville'—well, you can get Superman tee shirts anywhere."

Smiling strangely, he shook his head. "Not like this one. The logo's different. It's like the one George Reeves wore on the TV show when I was a kid. In my mind he's the one and only Superman. The original. And this is just the way the logo on his shirt looked."

"Are you crazy? All the Superman tee shirts look exactly alike."

"This one's different. It's like the one I had when I was a kid."

"Not that big, I'll bet."

He checked the size. "Adult. Large." Before she quite grasped what he was up to, he had handed money to the nondescript woman in charge of this "shop".

"You're not going to wear that?" his companion asked.

He was.

As they trudged to a snack bar he pulled off his tank top and pulled on the new purchase. "Look! Up in the sky! It's a bird! No, it's a plane!" He shouted the words, embarrassing her.

She persuaded him to stop shouting. They bought plastic cups filled with cold Pepsi and wandered away from walkways and bike paths and closer to the surf. After a while they both rolled up the legs of their jeans and went wading. Occasionally they had to run inland to avoid a particularly aggressive wave.

For a while they jogged, splashing and laughing, through the icy water—but as fog invaded the beach Jason's mood also darkened. Though they continued to stroll along the sand, always paralleling the distant shops and apartments, conversation lapsed.

The fog thickened. People rolled up blankets, gathered up surfboards, captured reluctant children. The beach became much emptier than one could have imagined.

"We'd better go," she said.

He walked on. She had to run to catch up. "Jason!"

"You go to the car," he told her. "I want to walk some more."

She shivered. Fog had grayed out the sun and was fast obscuring the Venice pier. Sprawling houses were dark blurs. The day had turned cold and dank.

"Go on," he said. "You've got gooseflesh. Go warm up in the car."

"Okay." She started in the general direction of the concrete walkway. Before she found it, Jason called out to her. She turned. He was a shadow in the swirling grayness.

"Jason?"

His sigh was loud enough to reach her. "You *like* your life, don't you? You like where you live...what you grew up to be..."

She did not know what to say.

Then he laughed, a brittle unnatural laugh. "Faster than a speeding bullet," he called, then turned away.

She watched a moment, and she understood that something needed to be said or done, but what that something *was* eluded her. By the time she made up her mind to go on to the car without him, the fog had worsened. A minute later she reached the firm reality of the concrete walkway—and stopped to look back. A churning blankness had obliterated the entire beach and ocean. The world ended a few feet away.

Except for one shadowy shape.

Not Jason.

Oh, no, not Jason. Not a man...

Much too large for that!

A twisting, bobbing thing, easily the length of a city street...

Then the fog hid it again and the young woman was shouting Jason's name into the emptiness.

THE ATTIC

Jeremy huddled against the raw wall, no longer mindful of splinters or spiders. At first he had been, but the multitude of battered cardboard boxes, ancient trunks, and discarded furniture proved hypnotic. One bare bulb suspended from rafters illuminated the attic and all its treasures. Dress forms here; scabbed, flaking canvasses there; an impossibly old gramophone; a crippled sideboard from Teddy Roosevelt's era; tarnished brass candlesticks too...

And, lurking everywhere, shadows, black, angry.

The boy did not notice the shadows. Hardly! A hundred other things vied for his attention.

Jeremy was nine years old. Small, indeed frail, he appeared younger. Dark eyes surveyed the world from a pale face; skittish, wary eyes that suggested brutality endured, a monstrous parent or older sibling tolerated without complaint.

Such was not the case. An only child, Jeremy suffered not brutality but adoration from a doting mother and father. They stifled him with their love.

So, today, this afternoon, this exact moment, the boy had sought escape, needing time alone for unscheduled, unsupervised fun.

Gramma's attic! A strange and secret place that invited an inquisitive child to poke and probe its wonders. Downstairs somewhere Jeremy's parents sipped tawny port and chatted with Gramma. But downstairs was another country. Up here were dust and cobwebs and freedom. No sounds either, except for the tattoo of rain on the roof. That and the boy's own breathing, muted and soft like a distant flute.

"You are now entering the Twilight Zone," Jeremy whispered, but the attic swallowed his words in its vastness. At random he selected the first container to pry open. In his imagination he was an archaeologist violating sarcophagi inside an ancient Egyptian tomb. "Some things are not meant to be tampered with," he intoned, the words ingrained from numerous viewings of the classic horror movies his dad collected. Not that Jeremy believed in, say, haunted houses or the undead, but he knew all about them from the movies. Evil souls unable to get to heaven and so still inhabiting the physical word, terrible beings filled with jealous rage against the living. Real scary stuff. But all make-believe.

The humpbacked trunk creaked in protest. He strained harder against the lid. "Doesn't want to open," he thought. "Boris Karloff's inside, all gauzed up in rot and bandages. Bet on it! He's in there, withered claws grabbing the inside of the lid, holding it shut! But I'm stronger! I'll break in!"

The lid would not budge.

Jeremy heaved against it until his face purpled and tendons stood out on his neck. Finally he sank gasping to the floor. The rain sang its lament. Shadows lurked behind torn sofas and unnoticed cartons. The overhead bulb dimmed a little.

Jeremy sat and considered the humpbacked trunk. No lock. No lock! Thing should have opened right up, easy as pie. Maybe the hinges had rusted over the years. Maybe the trunk was jammed shut.

Or maybe Karloff doesn't want to be disturbed.

So let the mummy sleep another thousand years, professor. Who cares? Plenty of other boxes to investigate.

Jeremy hunted awhile. Found a screwdriver in the rubble. With a vengeance he went to work. The humpbacked trunk groaned as the boy hammered the tool under the lid's lip, then thrust his weight against the screwdriver handle. "Comin' to get you, Karloff," he panted. "Gonna break you out! You bet I am, I am, I am!"

Metal gave. He levered with all his might.

And somersaulted over the trunk as the screwdriver snapped in two. Though the force of the fall was blocked somewhat by his flailing hands, his forehead smacked something–trunk, floor, mummy's fist! What did it matter? –and he was sure he was going to puke or cry or pass out or maybe do all three at once. Instead, he knelt there and put his head between his knees until the nausea and dizziness abated. "You lose," he thought. "Game's over. It'll take a nuclear bomb to get that thing open."

But he was a stubborn child. He knew he was. So did his parents. They called it "perseverance" and often bragged about that characteristic of his to relatives who couldn't have cared less. "Perseverance" was, apparently, something to be proud of. According to his grandmother, it ran in the family.

Only Gramma dared challenge the supposed value of this virtue. Once, quite a while back, she had mentioned some other child in the family who had been stubborn. Just who this was, what relation to Jeremy, had never been made clear. The other child had years and years and years ago, fallen headfirst into a lake or well or something like that. This, in spite of repeated prohibitions to leave the kittens alone. Jeremy was not certain what Gramma meant about kittens. Maybe the other child had attempted to save the kittens from drowning. But that explanation seemed somehow false...

Jeremy's mother had interrupted Gramma. Such stories were unsuitable for impressionable young boys! Gramma's scowl had served as the narrative's only conclusion.

When had Gramma told that tale? A couple of Thanksgivings ago? Yes, surely, a Thanksgiving–for Jeremy and his parents had been here in this huge house, visiting Gramma. He knew they had been here because of Gramma's bureau drawer. Hadn't he been exploring this three-storied house around the same time as the telling of the kitten saga? Hadn't he in fact snooped in Gramma's bedroom, rooted through her bureau, discovered that pink ceramic rose carefully wrapped in silk scarves? Yes, absolutely! A pink ceramic rose that wasn't a rose at all but a tiny container which hinged open to reveal a faded photograph. Even in grays and whites, the little girl had been movie-star perfect, with long luxuriant curls and a cherub beauty. And if her smirk had not hinted at some hidden wickedness concealed beneath the enchanting exterior, Jeremy would *still* have scraped at the portrait with his thumbnail until the face had been slit;

the little girl's beauty had infuriated him, for he had been cognizant of his own plainness. Later he had wondered if that little girl was the child who drowned.

Stubborn little girl. Wouldn't listen to warnings about kitties.

Well, he was every bit as stubborn. Only in his case it was good to be stubborn. Mom said so. "Persevering." That was the word.

Persevering!

No Egyptian sarcophagus that looked like a stupid humpbacked trunk was going to keep him out! If he wanted to uncover a long-lost mummy, he'd uncover that mummy!

Jeremy pondered his problem. Rain thrummed, the ceiling bulb dimmed perceptibly, shadows waited. Downstairs yet another Thanksgiving had come and almost gone, meal of rich foods consumed, wine bottles empty, adults satiated and lethargic. Up here Jeremy's memory of turkey, gravy, dumplings, cranberry, and pumpkin pie had long since died. He was a famous archaeologist and he would open that trunk! But how?

When it came, the answer was simple. Your screwdriver broke? So what? Your idea was okay, your tool puny. How about a better lever?

At that point his vision played a trick on him. Near a mildewing wing chair the shadows seemed to recede, to slink back, revealing what had hitherto been shrouded in darkness. A greasy, thick-looking crowbar. He blinked, but the crowbar remained, substantial and real.

He hefted it. Strong. Heavy. This would not snap in two the way the screwdriver had.

Delighted, he attacked the trunk. Levered the lid with renewed strength. Again metal yielded—this time the trunk's hinges. "Here I come, Karloff!" the boy gasped as he forced the lid up inch by inch. " Here I come, mummy, ready or not!"

The lid squealed and sprang open.

Boris Karloff was not inside.

The little girl was.

Like a rush of wind she flew up at him—her mouth open wide, impossibly wide, and filled with far too many teeth.

The shadows sprang forward an instant before the ceiling bulb blew out.

CONFESSION

Old Father Heron sat dozing in the confessional. It was almost nine o'clock at night and the church, vast with silence, seemed to hold its breath. The priest stirred and blinked awake. *Cold,* he thought. *Dank. Better move while I still can. Nobody will be coming here to Saint Mary's this late, not on a Saturday night. No, no, close up shop...*

But even as he squinted at the radiant dial of his watch—the confessional was dark as a sealed coffin this December eve—church doors squealed...and footsteps, reluctant, soft, approached. Father Heron groaned, settled back on the chair, offered these extra minutes as a penance for his own transgressions.

"Bless me, Father, for I have sinned." A man's voice, rapid, agitated. "It has been a long time since my last confession."

The priest murmured encouragement.

"Father, do you believe in ghosts?"

The question was so unexpected that Father Heron was momentarily speechless.

"Do you, Father?"

"What has this to do with—?"

"Do you?"

"Our Catholic faith enjoins us to believe in survival of the soul."

"I'm talking about hauntings, Father. Do you believe that the dead can torment the living?"

"Why would they want to?" The priest fingered his purple satin stole. "And, please, if this has something to do with your sins, I fail to understand."

The penitent sniggered, an ugly unpleasant sound in the anonymous darkness. "Oh, it has to do with the worst sins of all, Father—the sin of hatred, the sin of revenge."

Silence. The priest stirred uneasily. "What's it you've done, then?"

"Picture yourself so jealous of a friend that, after years of concealed anger, you murder this friend. You bludgeon him to death—dump him in a swamp. Can you also imagine the horror that comes afterward, when you are tormented day and night by the ghost of the man you killed?"

Father Heron stared into the darkness. "Murder," he whispered.

"Yes, murder—savage, pointless, stupid. And the body has never been found. No one knows."

The old priest took a deep breath and chose his next words with care. "You seek forgiveness, my son. To absolve you I must know your heart. Are you truly sorry for what you've done?"

The voice was a desperate moan. "Yes! Yes!"

"I believe you. Will you show this sorrow by deeds?"

Silence.

"My son, I will grant you absolution, but you must find the courage to confess to the police as well as to me. Your absolution is not dependent upon your going to the police, but you nevertheless should. Pray for the strength to admit this murder."

The man's voice was a cold wind. "My sin is not murder. I am guilty of hatred and revenge. Forgive me, Father, for tormenting the man who killed me."

SUDDEN MADNESS

That telephone call ruined an otherwise perfect Thursday night.

Feeling bloated and satisfied, Michael ignored the ringing and, sprawled on the living room couch, gulped a beer. "Will you get that?" he finally yelled, his thoughts still on a tour of taverns and old Jase Parker's retirement party. And what a party! Beery toasts, so many rounds of drinks that you were swimming, girls who couldn't be much more than eighteen kissing everyone in sight, and sixty-five-year-old Jase offering all his co-workers free grass...

The telephone rang and rang. Then Michael remembered that Marci was in the bathroom. With effort he hauled himself into the kitchen and pulled another beer from the refrigerator before grabbing his cordless phone from its precarious perch atop the wine rack. Reflected in the patio door's black glass, his own pale specter made Michael uncomfortably aware of the receding hairline, wild beard, and bulging stomach—all of which added years to his actual thirty-five. "Hello?"

"Mike, your sister's in the hospital." The voice belonged to Ross, his brother-in-law.

"Andrea? You're kidding! Is she okay? What happened? An accident?"

"She—well, she had a mental breakdown. God! That sounds awful, but there's no other way to tell you. I got back early last night for Billy's birthday and there she was, down on her hands and knees, pushing his brand new toy trucks. Well, that's not so strange. I mean, she always plays games with him. She's a real good mother. You know that."

"Ross, tell me what happened!"

"She wouldn't stop playing with the trucks. I thought she was putting me on. When I tried to make her stop, she started screaming. Wouldn't talk, not a word, just screamed and cried, until I got so scared I called our doctor."

As he listened, Michael returned to the refrigerator for another bottle of beer. The more Ross babbled, the shakier Michael felt, and soon the six-pack was depleted. Andrea–stable, levelheaded Andrea–in the *psychiatric ward*? Andrea, who had always been the one in his family with brains, with her masters degree and teacher training...

"Mike, listen!" Ross was almost sobbing. "I don't know how long she'll have to stay in that place. They've got to run tests. And I can't look after little Billy; I'm on the road for weeks at a time. Hell, I almost didn't get here yesterday. Can you imagine what might've happened if I hadn't? And Billy, so proud about being four years old, so proud! For weeks he talked about his birthday–'When's it going to get here, Mommy, Daddy, when, when?'–and Andrea told him he'd be such a big boy when he got to be four, and he'd be able to do all kinds of things a little three-year-old couldn't, and he was so excited, so proud. And then, yesterday, for me to come home and find Andrea that way! Oh, Jesus!"

If he had been sober, Michael would have sensed what was coming. At the moment, however, the kitchen floor was imitating a seesaw. "Can I help, Ross? Anything, man, I mean it. Hey, she's my sister!"

On the other end of the line, Ross began to blubber. "Please, please, can you take Billy for a while? Just a few days, until they let Andrea come home. There's nobody else I can turn to. I can't take time off from work. We'll need every penny with Andrea in the hospital. Please, Mike! Your wife doesn't work. She can look after Billy."

Too inebriated to think straight, he let his emotions respond. "Sure, we'll keep the poor little kid here."

"Billy's coming to stay with us?" asked his wife, Marci, after the call ended.

"Yeah. Tomorrow morning. Ross is driving him."

She nibbled her wedding band. "I'll be glad to look after him. But I can't believe you agreed to take him. You always say you can't stand noisy children."

With morning came the biggest hangover in years—and remorse. Not for the boozing, but for the lunacy of his decision. How would he ever endure days, perhaps weeks, of a little boy's raucous energy?

Little Billy arrived promptly at nine a.m. Ross, haggard, right eyelid twitching, led him by the hand from a white Toyota Corolla now blocking the driveway. "I really appreciate this," he told Michael and Marci. "His clothes are in this suitcase, and I've got his toys in the car. Just a minute..."

When he returned with the box a moment later, his arms shook.

"I'm glad you brought stuff for him to play with," said Marci. "I've got a collection of dolls in my bedroom, but I don't think they're quite his speed."

"Oh, he's at the stage where he'll play with almost any toy."

"You look like you could use a hot cup of coffee, Ross," she said. "I've got a fresh pot."

Ross rubbed eyes that looked dead. "Thanks, but I'm due in L.A. by ten."

"Well, I've got Styrofoam cups. Take some coffee with you." She hurried into the kitchen, while Michael wondered if he looked as aged as his brother-in-law did.

Little Billy grinned. "Uncle Mike," he said, his clear blue eyes a vivid contrast to his father's bloodshot ones, his big smile loving, "I'm *four* now!"

"Yeah, Billy, I know. Guess you got a lot of gifts too, huh?" Michael felt a pang of pity for this blond child in denim overalls and Mickey Mouse tee shirt who seemed so—well, trusting! Already the world had dumped its refuse on him. Andrea, in the funny farm! Happy birthday, Billy!

"First time he's said a thing since—" Ross left the sentence unfinished.

"I can do a lot of things I couldn't when I was three," Billy announced. "I like being four."

Marci was back with a steaming cup. "Here you are, Ross."

Wincing as the liquid scorched his lips, Ross gulped a mouthful and, amidst a flurry of kisses and handshakes, darted for his car, puddles of coffee marking his path. "Let you know soon as I hear anything," he hollered from the driver's seat.

And they were alone with Billy.

"I'm hungry," he said. "We didn't have breakfast."

Michael rumpled the boy's hair. "I'm late for work. Aunt Marci will make you something."

"Can I have strawberries?" the child asked.

"You're sure you can manage?" Michael feared a negative response from his wife. If she couldn't, he would be obligated to help. "I could call in sick," he suggested, not wanting to. So far the boy had been quiet enough, but how long would that last?

"I'll be fine," Marci assured him. "If there's anything I can't handle, I can call you at work."

"I love you," he declared, fervently. "You're amazing." He meant it, but even as he kissed this slender, almost frail woman, he shuddered with relief. If he'd had to cope with his nephew—much as he loved the boy—there might soon be two people in the psychiatric ward.

"I want strawberries," Billy said again, and tugged Marci's sleeve. "Mommy always gives me strawberries on my oatmeal."

"How about orange juice and scrambled eggs instead?"

"Buy me strawberries!" His tone hastened Michael from the house.

Once in his BMW, the beach house lost from view, he slowed from eighty-five to the legal limit and unrolled windows. No need for air conditioning yet; the morning was still cool, breezes ocean-fresh and unpolluted for at least another few miles. Smog awaited, along with city congestion, but for a moment he could inhale deeply and enjoy the scenery. Waves foamed, gulls circled in a Disney-perfect sky, joggers huffed across dunes, a teenage girl peeled her clothes for the day's first swim.

He reached into his shirt pocket for a pack of cigarettes. Thank God he was here, on his way to the office, and not back there trying to placate a shrieking four-year-old! Thank God for Marci!

At noon he called home to see how things were going. “No big problems,” his wife assured him. “Billy wants strawberries. Will you pick some up on your way home? We could use a pound of hamburger too.”

“Sure, okay. How are you and Billy getting along?”

“Oh, fine. He’s so cute! We walked to the beach with his toys, and he insisted on going in the water.”

“You mean wading?”

She laughed. “No, swimming. At first I wasn’t going to let him. After all, those waves can knock down people a lot bigger than he is. But he got away from me—believe me, he runs fast! —and the next thing I knew, there he was, paddling along like an old pro. He didn’t stay in very long, though. Too cold.”

Vague apprehension inched through Michael. “He swam? In that rough water?”

“Sure. Mike, what’s the matter? You sound—I don’t know...”

Michael’s frown deepened. “Billy doesn’t know how to swim,” he said, slowly. “Ross is afraid of the water. Wouldn’t let Andrea teach him.”

“Well, she must have, anyway.”

“Yeah, I suppose.”

“Don’t forget the hamburger. And the strawberries. Billy loves strawberries.”

“I love *you*, “ he said.

Ten-forty-two p.m.

His car swung into the driveway.

“We had to change those damn ads three times,” he complained. “The studio kept calling with last minute ideas. Can you believe that? This movie showcases next week, and they’re still tampering with the campaign.”

Marci nodded in sympathy. “Have you had dinner?”

“Yeah, around six. I figured we’d be stuck there forever. Oh, I did remember the meat and strawberries. See?” He displayed the grocery bag. “How’s Billy?”

“Dead to the world. That kid is a dynamo. We played hide-and-seek, tossed the beach ball, built sandcastles, ran races, played with his spacemen and trucks, you name it, we did it. You picked out nice strawberries, hon."

"Got any of this morning's coffee left?"

Seated at the kitchen table, they sipped from mugs Marci had made years before in art school. "Ugh!" She made a face. "This stuff's awful. What did I do wrong?"

"Tastes okay to me. Maybe there's something else in yours along with the coffee. Soap? You know how the dishwasher is."

"It's not soap. This coffee just plain tastes lousy."

He tried his again. "Coffee's fine. There has to be something in yours. Get yourself a clean cup."

Marci's lips contorted. He watched as she poured her mug's contents down the drain. "Let me taste yours, Mike."

He handed her the mug. Again she grimaced. "You don't think this tastes terrible?" she asked.

"No."

"Well, I sure do." Returning it to him, Marci moved to the refrigerator and rummaged.

He studied her thoughtfully. In ten years of marriage his wife had not gained a single additional pound—could pass for a teenager with those lustrous eyes, dark mane, and delicate beauty—whereas he now lugged a paunch to and from work. Too much sitting, too little exercise, and definitely too much drinking.

Marci was back at the table with a glass of Coke. "This tastes good."

They sat talking until Michael's yawns overwhelmed his comments. While he undressed, scrutinized by twelve grinning dolls that perched on his wife's vanity, Marci went to check Billy, only to reappear with one of her notorious midnight snacks.

"Want some?" she asked, extending the bowl.

Already half asleep, he groaned a reply. "No thanks. Why don't you gain weight? Always eating late at night..."

"I get plenty of exercise, hon." She swallowed another strawberry. When she spoke again, he was drifting into a dream. "Did I tell you that Billy's really bright? Wait till he's old enough to go to school!"

Really bright. Terrific. All he wanted was a little shut-eye, not a discussion of his nephew's I.Q.

"You didn't hear him, Mike. He didn't do it for you."

"Do what?" God, to get some sleep! This day had been everlasting. What relief that tomorrow was Saturday!

"Show off his vocabulary, that's what! He knows complicated words that most kids twice his age don't. And he's only four."

Wonderful, thought Michael.

"Sure you don't want a strawberry?"

But he was asleep.

All that night he was plagued by dreams. The initial ones involved his sister. Nothing horrible. Simply Andrea the way he remembered her, smart and athletic and charming. He watched her dive into a swimming pool and followed her off the board. But instead of surfacing to hot sunlight, he bobbed up through the carpet of the office where he worked. Computer screens fizzled and hard drives died, all his art work lost forever, while he raged helplessly and disembodied voices shouted, "Your ad campaign stinks! Fix it, fix it, fix it!" He staggered away from the failing computers and to his drawing board, gaped at the monster movie vampire pictured there, even as the voices shouted ever-changing standards he must meet. Suddenly the Bristol board illustration disintegrated into a jigsaw of confetti and he had to glue all the confetti together again before he could go home...

Inexplicably he was home, and Marci was outdoors, in the sea, floundering, her hair flowing like auburn tendrils as she struggled beneath the froth. Sand gripped his feet, and he was unable to rush toward the waves that pounded her deeper and deeper into darkness. Billy was there too, mouth stuffed with strawberries. "You can't assist her, Uncle Mike. You'd prefer to drink. Here, indulge in this gin and tonic. Calm yourself. You forget that I'm an expert swimmer. Why, I'm four now, and Mommy always promised I'd be able to do many things at this age. Watch while I demonstrate."

"You're swimming the wrong way!" Michael screamed. "She's back here! Back here!"

In a paroxysm of fear he leaped out of bed, only to gasp and squint at the fierce light intruding through the curtains. He groped on the nightstand for his wristwatch. Almost noon. A shrug and he had dismissed all memory of the dreams. Night whispers meant nothing.

"Marci?"

No answer. Well, what the hell? She had to be outside playing with Billy.

This surmise was verified when, garbed in jeans and a tee shirt, he shuffled barefoot into the kitchen and spotted her note on the table:

HOPE YOU HAD A GOOD SLEEP.
WE ARE GOING TO THE PLAYGROUND
ON A PICNIC. WOULD YOU LIKE TO
JOIN US?

He crumpled the paper but stopped short of the garbage can. Something about his wife's note seemed unusual. The words were hers, surely, and yet—

The telephone interrupted.

"Hey, friend, I hate to bother you on the weekend, but those bastards want the vampire layout changed before it goes to the newspapers."

"Again? Are they out of their minds?"

"They want it by Monday morning at eight."

Profanity would not alter the facts, so Michael settled for punching the refrigerator. *Jesus!* he thought. *And I wanted to call Ross today. Find out how my sister is. See if they're letting her have visitors at that hospital.* He had telephoned a florist yesterday from work, sent "get well" flowers; maybe he could squeeze in more calls today. No time now, though, not even for a quick breakfast. Writing a hasty memo for Marci and leaving it on the table, he was out the door.

Marci's note was in his pocket, its peculiarities forgotten.

In his worst premonition en route to the office he had not suspected that he and the others would be there until evening. Finally, at seven, Gary and Dave and he trudged toward the street.

"Some crappy Saturday, huh?" Gary snorted. "How about a quick drink, you guys, to celebrate the fourth version of that movie ad? First round's on me."

One round followed another and another. Before he realized it, eleven-thirty had come and gone and he had not called home. But he was feeling good, too good to curse the broken telephone in that bar or to sacrifice warm companionship for a pay phone elsewhere. And it certainly wouldn't be the first time he had gone drinking with his pals. Marci would understand.

When at last he did drop coins into the telephone in an all-night fast food restaurant, he hummed quietly and had no sense of foreboding.

Billy answered. "Oh, hello, Uncle Mike."

"What are you doing up this late?" Michael demanded.

Billy ignored the question. "I hope you've had dinner, Uncle Mike, because Aunt Marci ruined ours."

Michael frowned. "How could she ruin the dinner? Your aunt's a great cook."

"Perhaps that's true, but she set the oven at an incorrect temperature and burned the chicken to a cinder."

"Let me speak to her, please."

"She appears involved in a game. Perhaps later?"

"Billy, stop this nonsense and let me speak to her!"

"Sorry, but that isn't possible. Will we be seeing you soon, Uncle?"

"Billy! Put your aunt on the line this instant or I'll—!"

Billy hung up.

Even as he angrily punched in the number again, Michael marveled at the child's communication skills. Marci had certainly been correct when she'd said—

His index finger grafted itself to a telephone button.

Marci *had* said that, hadn't she? Last night, while he—weary from work—had lain in that twilight of semi-consciousness...

Yes. And—

Michael dropped the telephone.

Strawberries! Had she been snacking on strawberries? But she hated strawberries. Didn't they give her hives?

Seizing the telephone, he tried his home again. This time no one answered.

A strange dread propelled him from the restaurant. In the parking lot, while probing his pockets for car keys, his fingers found the crushed piece of paper. All the long miles to his beach house those words his wife had jotted on that paper careened before the car headlights.

Then he was there, finally, slamming to a halt, ignoring the keys in the ignition, his soft muscles straining as he bolted up the front walkway and through the open door.

"Marci?" he called.

From the living room couch Billy greeted him. He wore pajamas and held a magazine.

"You–you're looking at the pictures!" Michael stammered, his tone begging the boy to agree.

"Oh no, I'm reading the articles."

"That's impossible. You don't know how to read."

Billy tossed the magazine aside and scrambled off the couch. "But Mommy did. Mommy could swim and play the piano and do all sorts of remarkable things. Now I can. After all, I'm four."

Deep in the man's throat a sound began, guttural and agonized. From one room to the next he stumbled, his eyes wild. Marci was not in the house.

"I can't do it unless I'm with the person for a day or so," said Billy, happily. "Why, Uncle Mike, whatever is the matter?"

But Michael had lurched into the night. "Marci!" he shrieked. "Marci!" Fountains of sand flew in his wake. "Marci, where are you?"

Then he thudded to a halt and stared, his body swaying and a coldness creeping into his fingers. Numbly his right fist unclenched. The wadded paper fell unnoticed. His wife's note. *Printed in scrawled block letters.* The kind of thing a third grader might produce...

But Billy was not in third grade. He was much younger.

So it hadn't stopped there...

A few yards away, amidst a confusion of toy trucks and plastic spacemen, Marci's dolls moonbathed, their fixed smiles as guileless as Billy's.

"Marci!" Michael whimpered.

She was making mud pies.

BRING YOUR FRIENDS WITH YOU

September is the cruelest month. School assassinates summer, vacation dies, children march to classes in funereal shock. It was just June! July fireworks were yesterday! What happened to the county fair and the dog day eternity of August? School again? Cry for summer! It died too soon.

September is the cruelest month, and Willy knew this as all children know it. He knew it at the playground that first day back in spite of the hilarity and shoving and madhouse games of tag, for he was a spectator and not a participant. He assuredly knew it in the classroom.

"So you're Willy," grunted Mr. Lawson, the fifth grade teacher. "I've heard all about you, young man. Miss Rigothy told me."

Miss Rigothy had taught fourth grade.

Saying nothing, Willy simply watched Mr. Lawson.

"Sit down," the man muttered, his pudgy hand waving vaguely at a row of desks.

Willy sat down.

Moments later a fat girl who needed less perfume and more soap collapsed onto the seat directly in front of him.

Willy tried breathing through his mouth.

Mr. Lawson greeted late arrivals. He had smiled at everyone, even the fat girl. At everyone but Willy.

Willy found himself nudging the paper sack he had brought with him, poking it with his worn-out sneakers. Other children displayed new backpacks or shiny lunch pails beside their desks. He had an old paper sack with a defunct grocery store's emblem printed on it.

On the blackboard Mr. Lawson had scrawled his own name and, smiling with as much realism as a clown, blabbered on and on about what they would be learning this year. Willy winced. Mr. Lawson's voice affected him just the way chalk scraping shrilly on the board would have affected him. Why didn't the man stop talking? Please, God, make him stop talking!

But it was useless to ask God for anything. Nobody liked Willy, not even God.

"...So let's start with a review of our basic grammar," said Mr. Lawson with fake bravado. "Let's see what you remember from last year." He consulted his seating chart. "Melinda Boyer? Can you give us an example of a proper noun?"

Melinda could. Unfortunately, her example was a preposition.

Mr. Lawson strained to maintain his smile. "We'll try again," he said. "Give us an example of a proper noun, Marvin?"

Marvin suggested that the word "boring" could serve as a proper noun.

Mr. Lawson's smile became a rictus. "No, I guess we'd better ask someone else, Marvin," he managed.

Willy folded his hands on top of his battered loose-leaf binder and wished himself back in time—back to August or July, back to the hikes through the woods and the hidden cave he had discovered, back to the games of pirate and spaceman and monster that he had played all by himself, back to the tunnels he had imagined and those he had not, back to the days of the mason jars and grasshoppers and snakes and spiders and the myriad collection of new and exotic pets...

"Willy, I'm talking to you!"

Willy blinked up into the puffy face of his teacher.

"Willy, give us an example of a proper noun."

The boy grimaced. "Glet," he mumbled.

The teacher frowned. "Glet? Is that what you said? Glet?"

"Glet," said Willy. "That's a proper noun."

"And exactly what does the word mean?" demanded Mr. Lawson.

"Mean?"

"Yes, mean! To be a word it must have a meaning."

The class simpered. Ugly little Willy was in trouble! Ugly, stupid little Willy, the kid they all picked on. Good! Oh, good!

Willy shut his eyes. He wished it were summer. "Does Lawson mean something?" he asked.

The teacher reddened, while for a second time the class chortled. "Shut up!" Mr. Lawson roared at everyone. "This isn't funny!"

"A name's a name, " Willy said. "That's all. Glet is a name. I don't think it means anything. It's just a name."

When Mr. Lawson moved nearer, Willy shrank into his oversized tee shirt and faded dungarees. "Please leave me alone," he thought. "Just leave me alone." His left foot nudged the paper sack on the floor.

"Don't pull your little routines on me," said Mr. Lawson, whose flushed countenance hung mere inches from Willy's nose. "You may've been able to make poor old Miss Rigothy's life miserable last year, but I'm used to little boys who think they can raise hell in class and get away with it. Act your age, Willy, or you'll be sorry. Very, very sorry."

Willy bit the inside of his mouth to keep back anger. "Leave me alone," he thought. "Please! I never did anything to you."

But the teacher was not about to leave him alone. "Give me a real word, Willy. A real word that's a proper noun."

"Glet," thought Willy. "Glet or Zebbub or Stroth!" In the silent vaults of his mind he shrieked the names, shrieked them with all the defiance and frustration possible for a small boy to contain. But Mr. Lawson's visage threatened violence, and so Willy kept the words inside their vaults and muttered another answer instead.

"George Bush."

The teacher's apoplectic face withdrew with the speed of a retreating basketball. "George Bush," the man repeated loudly, so that anyone who had missed Willy's mumble would know what had been said. "Yes! That's a good example of a proper noun."

Willy sagged into his own skin. It was over. Now the teacher would leave him alone. Already Willy was back in that cave, pretending to be a pirate looking for hidden treasure—or maybe an astronaut fleeing Martian monsters deep within that planet's caverns. It did not matter, the game; it mutated every few seconds as he groped downward with his flashlight and the rocky tunnel continued to narrow and the descent became ever more difficult. He inched forward on his belly, and had no inkling of how much time had passed since running across that field of dead weeds, his bicycle abandoned, all but forgotten in his need to explore this field so far from his house. It was another tract of land like so many others he had passed, and yet it was something more. The wind told him. So did the tingle of his flesh. See what's here! See what's here!

Laughing, he had run in circles.

And then he had fallen. An unseen hole in the soil. And voices calling, maybe in his own mind or maybe not, voices urging him to seek, to find...

Find what? More snakes and lizards for his weird pet collection? He needed friends more than pets, friends who would like him and look out for him. But the voices made promises and the tunnel was the way...

"Willy!"

The tunnel was gone, replaced by the classroom. Mr. Lawson stabbed at Willy with a finger. "Willy! When I ask a question, I expect an answer."

Willy's little mouth trembled. "It's not fair," he thought. "I already answered a question. He should call on somebody else."

"Willy! I expect all my students to pay attention in class. Didn't you get enough sleep last night? Miss your nappy-poo, did you?"

Much to Mr. Lawson's satisfaction, the class tittered.

Willy looked hard at his teacher. "Leave me alone," he said softly.

Mr. Lawson loomed nearer. "What did you say?"

"Leave me alone!" Willy shouted it.

Hushed shock, followed by hoots of laughter.

"Shut up!" Mr. Lawson bellowed at everyone, moved even closer to Willy, and glared at the frail boy whose uncombed hair resembled so much hay and whose eyes glittered like blue pools of fire. "Who do you think you are?" the teacher sputtered. "Who the hell do you think you are?"

Willy's eyes dilated.

"I know all about you!" Mr. Lawson cried. "Miss Rigothy told me everything! Everything!"

Willy nudged his paper sack.

"You drove her crazy! She had to quit teaching! Well, you won't do it in this classroom, young man. Not to me! You'll behave with proper decorum—proper respect—or else!"

Again Willy shut his eyes. "Or else what?" he asked.

"Get up to that chalkboard! Right now! You're not going home until you have written one hundred times 'I will treat Mr. Lawson with respect.'"

Willy did not budge.

"Get up there! Or shall I call your father instead? Miss Rigothy said she did that. She said he thrashed you."

The class catcalled while Willy blushed.

Mr. Lawson exerted his full authority and yanked Willy from his seat. "Now, young man! The chalkboard!"

Willy opened his eyes. "Leave me alone," he repeated, his voce soft as a serpent's hiss. "Miss Rigothy told you a bunch of lies. I didn't make her quit teaching. I didn't do anything. She picked on me all last year. Every day, every single day she picked on me, just because I was different from the other kids. But I didn't do anything to her. I couldn't. I didn't meet Glet until school was already out for summer vacation."

The room rippled with nervous laughter. Willy, weak little Willy, the loser nobody liked, was not reacting the way he should. Weak little Willy was not intimidated by the hulking Mr. Lawson.

Mr. Lawson's head looked like a swollen purple balloon. He clenched his fists, wanting very much to strike at Willy's nasty little mouth. "All right!" he intoned. "All right! I'm calling your father today after school. Maybe another good beating is what you need!"

Willy released the blue fire in his eyes. It shot like oily death from a flame-thrower, but the teacher did not notice. "Go ahead and call my father," said Willy. "He won't do anything. He's afraid."

"Afraid? Of you? Should I be afraid, Willy?" The teacher's tone was mocking. "Should I be afraid of you?"

The fat girl—smelly, repulsive, a grotesque—pivoted in her seat and laughed in Willy's face, and it was this more than anything else that brought Willy's hands to the paper sack.

"Not afraid of me!" Willy whispered the words. "Not of me!" He fumbled with the sack, withdrew a large mason jar, unscrewed the lid.

"I shouldn't be afraid of you, Willy? I shouldn't be afraid of my little hell-raiser?"

Choruses of laughter from the students.

Willy's eyes shot blue flames.

"No," he said, face gleaming with a fine mist of perspiration. Then the lid was off the mason jar.

Mr. Lawson was enjoying the confrontation, now that the class laughed at Willy. "But you like to raise hell, don't you, Willy? Miss Rigothy warned me—"

Whatever else the teacher intended to say was lost in the searing flash of light and heat. Glet and the others hurtled forward on the wave of burning brimstone.

The teacher did not even have time to scream.

"Yes," said Willy, his words lost in the chaos of desks overturning and children shrieking. "I like to raise hell..."

CHILLING

For years they've told this story, usually at night after a few drinks have loosened tongues and felled common sense. *He's not really buried! He's frozen in cryogenic suspension at some Riverside lab!* Nobody actually believes such nonsense. But, still, it's fun to speculate. And if anyone had the drive and bucks to accomplish it, he did...

In a way the wild rumors do make a weird sort of sense. How, after all, did he make that ton of money to begin with? You know as well as I do. By being ahead of his time. By creating the world's first and most spectacular theme park. Sure, there have been carnivals and wax museums forever, I guess, but you can no more compare them to his conception than you can compare a kid's stick figure drawing to a Van Gogh.

You know the name of his amusement park. Everybody does. But consider what's in the park. *Future World,* with all those flying saucers and that simulated gravity-free space station—right next to *History World,* inhabited by Viking warriors, King Tut, Saint Patrick, Ben Franklin, Nero (costumed actors, one and all!)—and *Storybook World,* where hirelings in pussycat outfits chat with awe-struck children while knights in full battle armor fight fire-belching dragons that snort and growl and rasp.

Except, of course, the dragons don't snort or growl or rasp. Incredible illusion wrought by modern technology. And that's the whole point, isn't it? Before *he* and his technicians invented such life-like creatures, we would have scoffed at such a possibility. Today nobody scoffs. Other amusement parks in Southern California and elsewhere have imitated his robotic dragons and ogres, usually with little skill and laughable results, but his were the first and best.

So now you understand why this other story about the man got started. People figure that any guy who could do this stuff—well, that same genius might be able to use his wealth and staff of scientific types to work other miracles.

We all know he loved his amusement park—loved it with such passion that he spent all his time there. We also know he was scared of dying. The tabloids headlined it even during his own lifetime. And we know he was fascinated by cryogenics. Freeze the body immediately after death, thaw it years later when medicine is more advanced. In that future time the cause of death will be curable, damaged organs repaired, the corpse's arterial system drained of preservative and flooded with fresh blood, the body made alive once more.

Or so the scenario goes. There are a few folks immersed in big thermos chambers right this minute; liquid nitrogen in the outer cylinders keeps them in Popsicle condition. But that's as far as it has ever gone, most of us think. No one has figured out how to defrost them without rupturing all the cells in their bodies. Something about moisture in body tissues expanding or contracting violently during freezing and thawing.

Besides, most scientists don't have a clue how to resurrect the dead anyway. Not yet. So these few pioneers go right on with their icy sleep.

But...

What about *him?*

He was inspired, inventive, ahead of his time. Did he take a chance on cryogenics, maybe his own original version of it? Even knowing about the insurmountable problem of cells in the body bursting like swollen balloons, would he have insisted on being frozen? He died in the nineteen sixties. Is he currently reposing in some secret laboratory, awaiting scientific resurrection?

Or, when all is said and done, is he buried in some obscure little cemetery? Once the bar closes, most people would admit that this second idea is probably the truth.

Sure, they'd say, go to his amusement park, enjoy the talking pussycats, delight at the mechanical marvels too, as long as you understand that these marvels are tricks. His dragons are only robots. His pussycats are guys in costumes. One way or another, it's illusion. With all his insight and determination, that's all he invented. Illusion. And death is no illusion. With all his genius, the man is as dead as Abe Lincoln.

Maybe.

Be careful, though. Wave to the mechanical winged horse, hug the actor who is Saint Patrick—but don't get too close to the talking pussycats. True enough, they're costumed actors. But one of them totters like a broken marionette as he walks and smells like spoiled meat...

PLANTINGS

Gramma Hathorne's obsession was her garden. Anyone who strolled past the large fenced-in yard could not help but reach this conclusion. Just beyond the metal posts and chain-link wire lay the Garden of Eden. An infinity of tulips, roses, and exotic flowers! A plenitude of colors, shades, and shapes! And in the middle of it all, Gramma, kneeling as if in prayer. Some days she weeded, other days she watered, others she pruned. Gramma Hathorne, on her knees, with dirt-crusted gloves and sunbonnet and beatific smile...

Jennifer Lawrence, who lived next door, had turned six the previous month. She made a point of visiting Gramma Hathorne often. Exactly whose grandmother old Mrs. Hathorne was had never entered Jennifer's mind. As far as the little girl was concerned, Gramma was *everybody's* relative.

Whenever Jennifer shoved open the rusty gate, thereby announcing her intended visit by means of its angry metallic shriek, the elderly woman would peer from her present task in the garden, call a greeting, and rise—sometimes with difficulty—to her feet. After inquiring about Jennifer's parents and listening with rapt demeanor to Jennifer's chatter and gossip, Gramma would urge Jennifer to pick a variety of flowers to be taken home. This would be followed by lemonade and homemade cookies or cake.

Lately Gramma had also been permitting Jennifer to help with the plantings. It seemed as if the old woman was forever digging holes in the soil and inserting dry seeds. Jennifer wanted to plant dandelions, not Gramma Hathorne's idea of something to be cultivated, but Gramma had agreed, albeit with an odd smile. She had shown the child how the seeds were dispersed by the wind once a dandelion died, and how each flower released its flying seeds that were part of the actual flower itself. Jennifer picked a cotton-like dandelion from her own back yard—there were none in Gramma's—and, with suitable directions, separated a few of the seeds. Gramma gave her a small area in the garden for planting.

Jennifer was dutiful. She watered and waited, watered and waited some more.

One morning she awoke to the sounds of loud voices, the crackle of a police radio. To the window she padded, a snub-nosed redhaired little thing in green pajamas with Pooh Bear clutched under an arm. She had enjoyed a good sleep; yellow sunlight slanted through the blinds, clear sky predicted a wonderful day. Nothing seemed wrong with the world...

But the world would never again be the same.

From her window she watched the police, the ambulance attendants, and the stretcher that transported Gramma Hathorne from house to...

Death.

"Unconscious when they got there," Jennifer heard her father later say. "Stroke, probably. She never regained consciousness."

Jennifer understood what death was. Her kitten had been hit by a car. Death was when they dug a hole and put you in and covered you up. When the kitty had died, Jennifer had felt like one of her dolls, stiff and make-believe alive. This morning she felt the same way, only worse, much worse. Yes, she was aware of her own thoughts, and realized that she must really be alive because she could think about things, could see, hear, move—but Jennifer's limbs felt as if they did not belong to her while her skin felt like plastic, heavy and impervious to sensation.

The child spent much of the day in front of the TV, but it could have been a blank wall for all the attention she gave Road Runner or Daffy Duck. In the late afternoon she wandered to the front sidewalk, and from there to the fence and finally Gramma's gate.

A grating squeal.

But the announcement went unheeded. Jennifer walked with uncertainty into the yard. The garden and flowers were the same as ever.

At any moment Gramma would open the kitchen door, descend the back porch steps, and invite Jennifer in for fresh-baked oatmeal cookies. The hundreds of flowers were bright and cheery. They knew Gramma would soon come outdoors to water them.

It was not until she noticed the dandelions that Jennifer wept. They had sprung up overnight–and Gramma had not seen. The joy of their growth meant *nothing* any longer.

As she trudged listlessly from one dandelion to another, the straw sunbonnet drew her attention. Gramma's hat, beside her garden gloves, spade, and watering pot, there on the picnic bench. Jennifer circled the bench. At last she nerved herself to pick up the hat.

Blue bow, chalk-white straw fabric. How many times had Gramma worn this? Gramma had been born with this hat on!

Oh, Gramma...

There were even a few hairs from Gramma's head clinging to the inside band...

Gramma's hair.

Part of Gramma...

And slowly, like water making its way through dry earth, a tiny trickle of happiness worked its way through Jennifer's plastic skin and she became fully alive again.

She went about her task with efficiency. She even used garden gloves, exactly the way Gramma always had.

And the late afternoon sun offered its warmth and promise.

Every day after that Jennifer intruded on her late neighbor's property to water all the plants with Gramma's hose, weed one small patch, and hum happy tunes. There were occasions when her parents saw what she was doing, called it trespassing, and ordered her to stop. Jennifer agreed, and as soon as their attentions were elsewhere made her daily visit to the Hathorne garden. A week passed. Another. And another. Jennifer stuck to her work with a tenacity remarkable even in adults. She remained patient.

On a Saturday morning some four weeks later a fine mist of raindrops enveloped the neighborhood. Jennifer awoke early, a sense of expectation snapping her into instant alertness. *Something* was different! *Something* was happening!

She dressed quickly and with a minimum of noise. Descended to the downstairs hall. Unlocked the front door.

A smell of freshness was in the air, that good clean smell of spring. Jennifer hurried to the Hathorne gate. Both house and garden were aglow with a trillion shining particles of mist as sunshine broke through the cloud cover.

Entering the yard, Jennifer stopped. A rainbow had materialized. It began at the Hathorne porch and shot skyward. Its colors were no less inviting than those of the flowers, and in combination the effect was overwhelming.

Reds, yellows, violets, all amidst the intense green of lawn and now–blue sky. New growth was everywhere.

And the child's smile was as new as the newest buds on the roses.

She edged nearer the garden and her smile continued to grow.

When the dandelions had appeared, they had seemed to spring up overnight. Jennifer's latest planting had taken many more days to germinate–but she had never doubted. If dead stuff from a flower could grow, then so would hair. Choking on her own emotions, little Jennifer ran into the garden to hug Gramma.

AFTERMATH

The sky was gray, the wind too cold, and the boy shuddered in spite of the man-size parka he wore. *Hurry,* he thought. *Mom will be mad if you're late again.* But time had little meaning anyway. Dawn came on those clear days so rare now and shafts of sunlight announced when to arise and till depleted soil. Or hunger pangs woke you. Or the fury of weeks of rain. On the clear days you worked until nightfall. On overcast ones you worked until nightfall also. Always you worked.

The boy was ten years old, or so his mother said. He had been born in the ruins of a farmhouse. His father had died soon after; he could not even remember the man.

The boy quickened his pace. The wind slashed against his hand-me-down clothes, inflating the parka, flapping the fabric of his trousers. Mom's watery gruel awaited, as did another night of candles puffed out by drafts that snaked through a thousand cracks in the hovel of a farmhouse. But the gruel and the candles and Mom's angry interrogation would have to wait awhile longer. He must visit first.

Friends were a luxury few could afford. Even now, all these decades after ENDTIME, few women were fertile–indeed, few humans existed. Those babies born often died. Neighbors might be as near as the next city–or as distant as the past. Friends? Well, whom could you trust? Friends were known to kill you for a bowl of soup...a tattered blanket...

"Trust no one." This was the Greatest Commandment of All. "Trust no one."

Once, claimed his mother, there had been other commandments. This her mother had told her, though what exactly these other commandments had been no one knew.

"Trust no one." ENDTIME's commandment. So, ever alert, the boy scanned his surroundings. Devastation everywhere: pitted roads, gutted buildings, and blighted terrain. Few trees, fewer plants. Even weeds failed to grow. And no people. No animals. Not even a bird.

Once he had actually seen a bird—but that seemed ages ago. A mud-colored wren that flittered in drunken circles.

Nature's only song now was the wind.

A plaintive song, an eternal sigh of longing...

Friend...

He ached with loneliness. He loved his mother, yes, but this was not enough.

Friend...

"Trust no one," sang the wind. "Trust no one, boy, no one!"

He smiled then. More ruins awaited. And he would visit.

It took time to locate an opening big enough to squeeze through. The outer walls had long ago caved in, entombing her amidst the rubble. Miraculously, however, the roof had held firm, and she was safe. Curiosity had brought him here again and again—until, last week, he had found a way in.

The stench of mildew was everywhere. Little light penetrated the interior. The boy took no notice of these things.

He climbed over the mounds of fallen debris, broken glass, shattered statuary. Reached out a hand in greeting.

"Hi," he whispered. "I'm back."

And stood in silence, staring at the life-size statue. Who was she? He did not know. But the sad smile—the dark eyes—transfixed him. For the longest time he gazed upon the beauty of the lady in blue. Her foot, he saw, was crushing a serpent.

He stared.

And smiled.

WOMAN IN THE FOG

It was nearing six a.m. as Jennifer Wu laced her running shoes, slid a sweatband over her forehead, and began the obligatory stretching exercises there in her second-story Venice apartment. Roommate Linda was not yet up, so Jennifer tried to be as quiet as possible. If anything troubled Jennifer, it was the fog she had noticed from the bedroom window. Fog made her morning run on the beach a waking dream—endless swirls of white nothingness instead of a breathtaking view of the sand and ocean at sunrise. Of course, fog was not uncommon. When it came, it came quickly. And it did hide the sleazy walkway with all those second-rate bric-a-brac stands and third-rate hustlers, so maybe it wasn't so bad after all.

Actually, though, Jennifer enjoyed the soiled, almost carnival ambience of the beach. Sure, drug pushers competed with mimes for your attention, at least after the crowds arrived each day and the tee-shirt stands opened and the skateboarders with their ghetto blasters swerved into view, but Venice, California was an exciting place to live. Who wanted dull routine anyway? Commuting five days a week to an insurance company job in Los Angeles was enough of a rut for anybody.

Jennifer stepped to the outside landing, locked the apartment door, and then locked the hinged metal grating that further sealed off the outdoor steps from the upstairs porch. Two different dogs barked as she made her way down the steps and across the sidewalk to the front gate.

Ten minutes later she had reached the actual beach. Fog, while present, was less formidable than she had feared. Perhaps she could enjoy a spectacular sunrise after all.

No premonitions, no sense of impending dread.

Jennifer Wu began to jog, gray sweat suit matching the gray mist.

Her waist-length hair streamed behind her. Her stride was easy, practiced, her breath controlled. She had, after all, been jogging here for nearly two years and was in good physical condition.

The wet sand squished beneath her Nikes. She made a point of always running close to the water. Better traction than on dry sand and much more scenic.

They say you should never jog alone on a beach early in the day or late at night. Too much can happen. Too many crazies loose.

Jennifer Wu had taken several self-defense courses.

Besides, she was not alone.

Five minutes into the routine she realized that someone was behind her. It was at this time that the fog intensified, roiling in from the water like some incredible alien atmosphere. Recalling a low-budget horror film she had seen on TV while a child, Jennifer smiled. The Crawling Eye. In that movie, fog had enshrouded a mountain road, even as monsters from another planet lay in wait for their next victim. The monsters had needed their own world's atmosphere to breathe, hadn't they? Yes, and the movie director had needed that silly fog to hide the fake-looking beasts until the last possible second.

Jennifer glanced over her shoulder. No sign of anyone. But some sixth sense suggested that this real-life ocean fog concealed its own real-life secrets.

She fancied she could hear steady footfalls matching her own.

Just another jogger. No big deal. Lots of people jogged on this beach.

Perhaps it was the fog that sent the first shiver of apprehension through her. There was no reason to be afraid, and yet she inexplicably was.

She quickened her pace. Glanced over her shoulder once more. And saw a figure emerge from the whiteness for one heartbeat before the mist blotted it from view.

A woman clothed in a gray sweat suit similar to her own.

But something was wrong with this runner's face.

Jennifer Wu, who prided herself on self-defense skills and a rational view of the world, found herself panicking. Terror broke the rhythm of her stride. She stumbled, choked, then bolted in blind flight away from the wet sand and her normal path. All sense of direction vanished in the fog. *Get away from the churning surf! Get away from that woman in the gray sweat suit! Run! Oh God, run!*

Time stopped. Jennifer blundered across dry sand and almost fell when the sand unexpectedly gave way to the concrete bike path. Then she was safe because, up ahead, buildings peeked from the blankness and she could see the street leading away from here and, yes, there were people, normal everyday people, and not a one of them in a gray sweat suit, not a single solitary one...

Except Jennifer herself.

Panting more from fear than exertion, she trudged the several blocks to her apartment. She failed to see the church she passed or the gang graffiti spray-painted here and there. In her mind was that figure in the fog.

That figure with garments saturated by ocean slime...

That figure whose face was a mass of putrid rotting flesh...

That figure who nevertheless was Jennifer Wu!

She had recognized herself in that horror that dripped of the sea and jogged behind her in the fog.

What did it mean?

The answer arrived later with the evening's local TV news. Police had apprehended a deranged man that same day, early in the morning, on Venice Beach. He had been found standing near the water and watching the waves wash over his victim, a young woman in her early twenties, who had been picked at random and shot repeatedly. She had been jogging.

That could have been me! Jennifer thought—and then realized it would have been her if that phantom figure had not intervened. Jennifer had seen herself as a corpse and been frightened into leaving the beach. Had she continued her usual run—well, Jennifer shuddered at the consequences...

THE WRITING ON THE WALL

Four-thirteen on a dreary afternoon in September—and Rodney Smith, age seven, was bored. What little homework teacher had assigned was too uninspiring to contemplate, the DVD player was broken, and Rodney's back yard was awash with flowing rivers of mud. No decent TV, no outdoor games, nothing! Rodney pressed his nose against the windowpane and studied the rivulets of water rushing from Mrs. Koslowski's gutters. Her house was upon occasion a pleasant stopover station on his interplanetary excursions—a sanctuary of Old World cakes and strange but savory cookies.

Not today. No visiting her. That house might as well be as far away as Saturn or Mars. Mama had spoken. "Stay inside, Rodney. You'll catch pneumonia if you go out in this."

So the afternoon dragged. A turtle on crutches would have moved faster. Currently occupying his own bedroom—he had driven Mama crazy while downstairs, too much whining and complaining—Rodney stood amidst a heap of coloring books, spacemen, crayons, comics, you name it, and was bored, bored, *bored.*

The room glowed in several spots, pools of light from a bureau lamp, a ceiling bulb. But there were shadows too, great splotches of darkness, and these added to the boy's gloom.

He finally picked up one of his coloring books—all about Batman—and, squatting on the floor, began a desultory job of crayoning.

Batman and Robin. Cartoon heroes, sure. Make-believe stuff. He knew that. And yet...

At least they were big people. They were grown up, adult, could go where they wanted and do what they pleased. Imagine Bruce Wayne's mother telling him not to go out because it was raining! Bruce Wayne would laugh as loud as the Joker. Gotham City always had lots of crooks, and Batman hunted them down, rain or no rain.

Yeah, it would be wonderful to be all grown up like Batman. Rodney scratched his nose wistfully, then added raindrops to the picture in the book—an illustration of Robin. Robin also was old enough to do whatever he wanted, including going out on rainy days.

The more Rodney considered his misfortune the more vexed he grew. He tossed the coloring book into the shadows and stood glaring at his reflection in the mirror above the bureau. The tow-headed, pudgy-faced image glared back, brow furrowed, mouth a tight slash. Construction paper art taped to the mirror's frame failed to lessen the bitterness radiating from that glass—from Rodney. Pirate flag, Yankee pennant, last year's funny valentine—all overloaded the mirror but were no longer bright or cheerful.

Without quite planning it, Rodney found himself staring at the child-size desk that was also reflected in the mirror—and at the photograph of himself perched atop it. He spun around, faced the actual desk, his fingers crushing a crayon he still held into the palm of his hand. As though mesmerized, the boy moved toward the desk, his gaze never wavering from that five by eight-inch photograph displayed in its cardboard frame. Rodney Smith, pasty and smirking, looking younger than ever, looking a thousand years away from Batman maturity—from adulthood's independence.

The flesh-and-blood Rodney seized his counterpart—slashed at it with the red crayon—scarred, disfigured the face—scribbled over it with a savageness that eventually broke the crayon. Rodney slammed the photograph flat against the wall behind his desk and ground the broken fragments of red into his paper duplicate. "Hate you, hate you, hate you," he breathed.

He stopped, all anger spent. Bits of crayon fell to the floor.

The first emotion to replace his rage was fear. This photograph Mama liked so much that she had purchased copies for all the relatives—ruined! Hide it, quick, quick!

Fear became total panic when he noticed the wallpaper. In his fierce onslaught he had overshot the target several times. Looking like so many half-healed scars, red streaks marred the pale blue wallpaper.

In a frenzy, Rodney stuffed the photograph inside a Fantastic Four comic book and buried the comic under a pile of others, all of which he lugged to his toy chest and abandoned. Back in front of the desk he froze, heart trip-hammering. Mama would see the marks on the wall. Mama would *see!*

Unless he could get the crayon off...

But how?

The bathroom!

He flew from room to room, grabbing a washcloth and cake of soap, soaking the cloth under the tap, hurry, hurry!

The smell of roast beef drifted into the hall. Downstairs Mama was busy with supper preparations. Make her stay busy, God, please!

Rodney lathered the washcloth with Ivory, dabbed experimentally at the wallpaper. No result. Red scribbling had become a permanent part of the wallpaper's design.

More soap! Rub harder!

Rodney worked with a gusto born of desperation. The blue wallpaper began to lose its blueness. The crayon smeared somewhat but kept its vibrant color.

More water, maybe? Wet the cloth again!

It took less than fifteen seconds to get to and return from the bathroom. But things had changed during this interval. Rodney looked for a long time at the wall.

The crayon marks had spread. The lines were longer. He was sure of it.

Better stop scrubbing. Must be streaking the crayon marks by rubbing...

Somehow.

Cover up the marks instead! Yeah! That was the answer!

He ran to the mirror, yanked down one of the larger construction paper masterpieces—a drawing of a robot—and thumbtacked it over the crayoned wallpaper, after first drying the wall with the sleeve of his shirt.

Good! Perfect! You could never tell there was anything wrong.

At supper he was abnormally silent and picked at his food. Later his mother played Candyland with him, but he remained distracted and irritable.

And why wouldn't he be irritable? Wallpaper boasting a dreadful secret, stupid photo bloodied and entombed in a crypt of comic books...

"It's the picture's fault," he thought. "I hate being so baby-looking!" So of course he had been forced to strike out at the offensive photograph. It made perfect sense.

But Mama would never understand. And sooner or later she would notice the absence of that photograph atop his desk. Sooner or later she would discover the crayoned wallpaper.

As he undressed for bed he tried to ignore the robot drawing thumbtacked above the desk. And he succeeded. It was not until Mama had tucked him in and turned out the lights that he at last gave in and looked. Outdoors a drizzle still fell and there was no moon, but the neighbors' house-lights provided enough illumination to reveal, however dimly, the desk and other furnishings.

Rodney squinted, peered, frowned, sat up, blinked—and jerked rigid.

There in the shadows and silhouettes of the bedroom were the desk and robot picture—yes, certainly, plain enough—but what else? What else was there, easing out from beneath the construction paper drawing, peeking at him, just beginning to venture across the wall like some kind of impossible worm?

The horror of the word *worm* grew in his mind until he could scarcely breathe. Rodney wanted to scream but his mouth seemed stuffed with Kleenex, his tongue a dead leaf.

When the *thing* crept farther along the wall he lunged for the flashlight on the chair beside his bed and clicked it on. He swung the beam, centering it on the robot picture.

Nothing. No red worm crawling from beneath the picture. Nothing.

He turned off the flashlight. Took a deep breath. Lay back. Closed his eyes.

Rain thrummed the roof. Boards creaked. Wind muttered.

Keep your eyes shut. Don't look. Go to sleep.

Slowly, very slowly, he sneaked open an eye. Only one.

And *thought* there was a blur of motion as something streaked back to its place of concealment beneath the construction paper.

He used his flashlight again. All was as it should be, but Rodney's heartbeat did double-time for many minutes afterward. He left the flashlight on, clutching it to his chest as he leaned back on his pillow.

And still nothing. Rain cascading off window glass, a shutter banging somewhere, nothing more, nothing unexpected. He tried to remain awake and vigilant, but soon the rhythmic night noises lulled him into a restless sleep.

The flashlight batteries, already old and much used, weakened and gave out. The bedroom was dark once more. Infested with darkness. And with something more.

Rodney snuffled, moaned, and dreamed. In his dream he had been taken fishing by someone. The identity of the "someone" remained uncertain because Rodney could not see this individual. That was not important. What was important was the rowboat in which Rodney sat, the strong bamboo fishing pole in his hands, the heat of the sun on his face and bare arms. The boat sat motionless on a wind-free lake. In the bright blue water tiny fish nibbled at the bait. Rodney felt himself smiling.

Then the biggest eel in the world had taken the hook and Rodney was fighting to stay aboard the rowboat. With dizzying speed the eel veered left, right, then back toward the boy. An instant later the eel was circling the rowboat and Rodney was ensnared in the unbreakable nylon line. The thin strand bit into his flesh, spun him round and round, until he was little more than a spool collecting thread. He shrieked at the stiff waxy texture of the constraining filaments...

And opened his eyes. His bedroom was darker than ever, but he was safe. A dream. Only a dream. His pulse slowed, though perspiration still trickled from his scalp.

Gradually he became accustomed to his surroundings and the nightmare receded. His vision shifted from ceiling to toy chest beneath the window. Yes, only a bad dream...

But from the corner of his eye he detected something awry. He was puzzled a moment—and then totally awake. Dark lines radiated from beneath the robot drawing, lines that he knew would be red if a flashlight beam spotlighted them. The lines extended from the wall by the desk to the wall beside the bed. And down. Down to the bed itself. Across the sheet and pillowcase.

Rodney wanted to scream. Wanted to holler that he had not really meant it when he obliterated his photographed face.

But Rodney could not scream. In fact, Rodney could not even move. Waxy tendrils of red had encircled his limbs and body again and again, had crossed out his mouth, and were now creeping toward his nose and eyes...

MY LADY

Andrew Delane arrived in California with little money but many hopes. His world was one of kerosene lamps, men who wore starched collars to church, and women who shrouded ankles in petticoats and voluminous skirts. This was a time when land was cheap. With a loan from relatives he bought a house.

For several years this medical man lived a bachelor's existence. He devoted his days to the sick, treating everything from measles to broken bones, his compassion and skill quelling doubts some might have voiced over his youth. He was also willing to help sick cows and horses. This more than any other trait endeared him to the community. He was not "highfalutin" the way some physicians were. From Massachusetts he might be, but Dr. Delane deserved respect.

Farmers became his friends. Their wives baked him pies, gave him preserves. And many a daughter gazed longingly, for he was tall and handsome, with finely wrought features, curly blond hair, and a ready smile. "How lonely he must be!" they thought. "How dreadful to return every evening to an empty house with no one waiting but a cat!"

The cat, it must be admitted, was a splendid beast, all black save for green eyes so bright that Delane sometimes fancied the animal's intelligence to be extraordinary. Often he would pet the cat and murmur, "So, My Lady, do you truly comprehend my words? What goes on in that small brain of yours? " And My Lady would rub her head against his knuckles and he would laugh at his own odd whims—for what cat can think or reason?

My Lady was certainly not human. But she loved him in a fierce feline way. She was his shadow whenever he was home. If he sprawled in an armchair, she sprawled on his lap. If he wandered the grounds, she danced at his side. When he slept, she curled beside him. My Lady had journeyed all the way from New England with him. She had always been his. If purring is proof of joy, then My Lady had been happy all her life.

One hot June night Dr. Delane introduced a newcomer into the house. Her name was Sarah, and she was his bride. Their marriage had resulted from a whirlwind courtship, aided and abetted by Sarah's father, a simple farmer who viewed any doctor as a true prize.

Sarah was eighteen, small and pretty in a freckled outdoorsy way. She sang to herself as her new husband lit the kerosene lamps and then poured wine into long-stemmed glasses. "To the only woman I've ever loved," he said with true sincerity. And she replied, "I'll love you the rest of my life."

"To the rest of our lives!" he exclaimed.

From atop the sideboard green eyes watched. They glittered with intense displeasure.

The doctor and his bride finished their wine and made their way to the bedchamber.

My Lady sprang from the sideboard but the door closed before she could follow them. For a long while she crouched in the hall and stared at the bedchamber door.

A sound came from the cat. Not purring. Hardly that.

The door remained shut.

My Lady screeched in anger and frustration.

No one let her in.

When she moved it was with purpose, and she was agile and rapid and sure.

By the time help arrived, the house was engulfed in flame. Heat drove back the bucket brigade. There was nothing they could do.

"Dear heaven," groaned the brigade captain, "Doc must've knocked over a kerosene lamp."

Actually most of the kerosene lamps had been knocked to the floor.

My Lady, who had escaped through an open front window, rubbed against the captain's legs. Her purring was loud. Almost as loud as the screams from the house.

FINAL EXAM

Gray walls; gum-spotted green carpeting; overhead fluorescent lights, one of which was dead; ceiling ventilator straining to pump in peculiar smelling cool air. And of course traps, twenty of them, trapezoidal-shaped tables with black cylindrical legs and graffiti-laden wooden tops. The forty plastic chairs were empty, their mustard color startling.

June 19, a Thursday, and the high school was devoid of students. Mr. Logan, English teacher, sat at his desk and brooded. Faculty members were required to put in this additional day, though the students had taken the last exams Wednesday and—for the seniors—graduation had been held at the stadium the previous evening. Mr. Logan's scantron tests had long hours ago been run through the machine, scores recorded in the grade book, scan sheets completed with final averages. File cabinets had been put in order, classroom walls stripped of posters, and student portfolios stored in cardboard boxes until September. All this had been accomplished by late afternoon yesterday, so today Mr. Logan was simply marking time, waiting for noon when he would be permitted to turn in his keys and go home.

The Language Arts Building—his department's home—was silent except for the hum of air conditioning and the occasional clicking of the Simplex wall clock. No P.A. crackled to life with special announcements. No administrator, or fellow teacher for that matter, stopped by to chat.

Hardly. The campus was deserted this hot California morning. Principal, counselors, instructors, secretaries were all at the Runway Plaza Hotel, no doubt gushing good cheer as they lurched around and around, socializing with colleagues they ordinarily detested, guzzling their so-called "End-of-the-Year Breakfast". Bloody Marys tended to replace pancakes, and the Runway catered to such excesses each year. Faculty and staff would weave back to campus by noon.

Mr. Logan enjoyed a drink as much as most, but he did not enjoy the taste of alcohol at eight in the morning. He also disliked the idea of driving back to the high school while trying to focus bloodshot eyes. And, truth to tell, it was fun to flaunt conformity. He did so on a regular basis, much to the annoyance of his supervisors. If everyone were expected to go to the breakfast, then he would not. As a result, he was alone on campus, because of an insane Board of Education policy that stipulated you either attend the faculty breakfast or be in your classroom by eight A.M. Though tempted to defy that policy and float in around the same time as the revelers, he dared not, simply because there was every chance some administrator would conduct a surprise visit to his room. Face facts! Administration viewed him as a pain in the ass, contentious, moody, impossible to work with, and had recently warned him to mend his ways or else. They would like nothing better than to add more black marks to the file he was sure they were keeping. "Empty classroom? Mr. Logan's gone? Not at the party, either! I just came from there. Have to write him up again. Overt defiance." In truth his record was at best already spotty. Too many days off, missed faculty meetings, no-shows for adjunct duties, complaints from parents over disparaging remarks targeting their kids. He did have tenure (the result of careful fawning the first three years of his academic career) and so was relatively safe, but he could "for cause" be dismissed, though such an action was rare, difficult to achieve, and required much documentation along with an actual hearing. But they were without question gunning for him. Best to be careful, at least until the administration tired of keeping him under their microscope.

And so he sat in a room without windows, sport jacket discarded on this last day, old jeans and running shoes and tee shirt replacing the usual attire. He sat, and after a while the unnatural quiet made him uneasy and his brooding increased. Why had he wanted to be a teacher, anyway? The salary was pathetic; he was treated like some sort of trained monkey by the administrators; classes were overcrowded and lazy and rude...

He rubbed his forehead. *"You're pushing forty,"* he thought, "and what have you got to show for it?"

As if on cue, the classroom door burst open and a large youth swaggered in. "I'm here for the test," he blared.

Mr. Logan's brow furrowed. He had never seen this kid before. "Test?"

"Yeah, test! You know—the final exam, man!"

"You must be in the wrong room," declared Mr. Logan. But as he said this he realized his own mistake. All examinations were finished as of yesterday. Unless this kid had received permission to take a make-up. "I'm not the one you need to see. I don't know anything about other teachers' make-ups."

The youth drew closer, a strange and unpleasant smirk on his otherwise unremarkable face. "You're the right teacher, Logan," he said softly. "It's time for the final exam."

Mr. Logan rose from his chair, but whatever indignant answer he had been about to make died in his mouth as his own gaze locked with that of the intruder. "It's like looking at a store mannequin," the teacher thought. "There's nothing going on behind those eyes. They don't shift or move. The irises don't expand or contract."

Which was absolutely impossible.

If this person were alive.

But of course he was alive! This was not some kind of Poe story! This was real life!

Nevertheless, Mr. Logan's saliva evaporated inside his own mouth and a coldness enshrouded him. With growing fear he studied the intruder. Big kid, built like a varsity football player. Short colorless hair, dead eyes, sweat shirt, jeans, work boots. Could be anybody from the senior class. Mr. Logan did not teach seniors, did not know them from their stint in junior year English either, was terrible with names, blended faces soon after September students replaced June's...

"Maybe he was in my class last year," the teacher thought. "Surely I recognize him, don't I?" But he did not. "Who are you?" he asked, the words difficult to form. "What do you want?"

The dead eyes never changed position.

"What is it you want?"

Again that awful smirk. "I'm here for the final exam."

"What are you–?" Mr. Logan made an effort to lower his voice, to eliminate the telltale panic in his strident tone. "What are you talking about? What final exam? Who are you?"

And still that smirk. "Exam starts in two minutes. Better sit down and get ready."

Mr. Logan's anger was sudden and decisive. "*I'm* not taking any exam. As for you, you're getting the hell out of here right now. Unless you want me to call security." He moved toward the corner where the white telephone hung.

"Go ahead. Call. There's no one in the main office. Matter of fact, there's no one on campus. You of all people should know that, Logan. You work here, not me."

Mr. Logan swung away from the telephone and started for the door. The trapezoidal tables forced him to take a roundabout route, but the heavy-set student made no effort to intercept him. Thank God! For the teacher was certain that this kid must be under the influence of some drug. Big mistake to confront him! Get out as fast as possible and look for help. No telling what the kid might do...

"One minute 'till test time. Take your seat, teach."

Mr. Logan had reached the door. But somebody was there in the hall waiting for him. A tall thin gentleman with snowy hair combed straight back from his forehead, black-framed glasses, dark suit, and maroon tie so narrow it immediately brought to mind an earlier decade.

As well it should. This man had been Mr. Logan's math teacher in high school.

"Mr. Bigelow? *Mr. Bigelow?"*

The newcomer winked. "I'm delighted you remember me."

"Remember you?" thought Mr. Logan, wildly. "Of course I remember you! You were my favorite teacher. Somehow or other you made calculus interesting. I didn't become a math teacher myself, but you inspired me to want to teach. My reason for going into this profession was you...*but....*"

Yes, Charlie Logan, come to grips with it. This man can't be Mr. Bigelow.

Beyond all sanity! Beyond all belief! And why, Charlie Logan? You know the answer to that, too. Bigelow retired the year you graduated from high school.

And?

And... a couple of years later this same Arthur Bigelow died. Remember? *Remember?* You read the obituary, saw his photo in the newspaper, and were moved to tears.

This man who stands here before you is rotting in his grave!

"Please sit down," said Mr. Bigelow. "It's time to start your final exam." Striding into the room and opening his battered leather briefcase, the calculus teacher withdrew a sheaf of papers. "This test is oral, Charlie. I'll ask some of the questions, but so will some other individuals also. Take your time in responding. Take as much time as you need. You want to pass this test, Charlie. You truly want to pass this test." Behind the glasses, Mr. Bigelow's eyes were as dead as marbles.

"This can't be happening!" Charlie Logan moaned. He sank upon one of the plastic chairs. From another area of the classroom came a shout of laughter. Cold, pitiless laughter. Logan twisted in his seat. "Who are you?" he cried miserably. The youth continued to laugh.

"He's no one," said Mr. Bigelow. "He's no one–and everyone. You'll see, Charlie. All in good time. And we're behind time, Charlie. Let's begin." He glanced at the papers in his hand. "First question: Are you a good teacher?"

"Wh-what?"

"I'll repeat it. Are you a good teacher?"

"Yeah, sure. Look, what the hell's this all about? You can't be Bigelow."

"Your response is that you are a good teacher. Is that correct?"

"Yes, sure. Hey, listen–"

"*Why* are you a good teacher, Charlie? Please elucidate."

The tone of the questioner's voice chilled Logan. He stopped protesting and sought a reasonable response. "Well, I'm good because I know my subject matter. I'm good because I've studied and developed expertise in my field."

"This isn't a job interview, Charlie. I'll refrain from insisting you prove that statement. No demands for information about Melville or

Hawthorne or their tiresome works. After all, mathematics is my field. I must take you at face value on your claim of expertise."

"Dammit, I know my stuff!"

Mr. Bigelow adjusted his glasses. "You probably do. But, tell me, Charlie, is that all there is to your answer? You're a good teacher because you 'know your stuff'?"

The classroom was icy. Logan could see his own breath and was more afraid than he had ever been in his entire life. His fear transcended the obvious causes. Yes, this had to be a nightmare; Bigelow was dead! Yet the ultimate fear came not from this fact but from the interrogation, the "final exam". Logan sensed the urgency behind Mr. Bigelow's admonition to pass. *What would happen if he failed?*

"I'm...uh...I'm a good teacher for other reasons too."

"Go on."

"Well...I try to help my students. You know, make the course relevant so they'll be motivated to study."

Mr. Bigelow was watching the third occupant of the room who stood somewhere behind Logan. "And do you motivate most of them, Charlie?" Mr. Bigelow asked.

"Most of them? Yeah." Logan could not help himself. He pivoted in the chair to see why Mr. Bigelow kept staring.

The student's face! It melted, coagulated, melted again, features shifting, altering, one face changing into another and another and another at a speed so rapid that Logan barely had time to recognize one before the next replaced it. A kaleidoscope of young faces, some with names Logan could still call to mind, others familiar but the names lost somewhere in the past. Freckles and a pug nose—Jerry McGrath—blending into pretty Michelle Lindquist—melting into that kid with the pout from three years ago (What was the name?)—fusing, changing, changing! A hundred faces or more, accusing, belligerent; faces of those he had never reached, who had hated school—and who hated him...

"I tried!" he exclaimed. "I did everything I could!"

"Did you?" inquired one of the faces. It laughed and the laugh rose up and down the scale as the countenances continued to change.

"I did!" he protested. "I'm a good teacher! I care about my students!"

The youth who was nobody and everybody stopped laughing. His visage stabilized a moment, became that of Arnold Nguyen—eyes bulging, neck twisted, flesh black from the noose. "So depressed! Such awful problems! I needed help. I came to you. You told me to talk to my parents. You told me you had papers to grade. I went home and fastened a rope to the garage rafters."

"I did have papers to grade!" Logan shouted. "Dammit, I had ninety term papers! I'm not a shrink! I'm not a priest! I'm just a teacher."

Another face. Jenny Johnson, the tenth grader who had overdosed on drugs. "I was in your class. Couldn't you see I was always putting my head down? Couldn't you see I needed help?" And another. Ted Conroy. "I kept drawing pictures of naked women on my book covers. You saw me. Didn't you guess I'd go out someday and actually kill a woman? Didn't you see the knives in my sketches? Why didn't you tell someone before I did it? Why didn't you stop me?" And then there were so many voices, so many half-forgotten students, so many accusations that Logan screamed to drown them out.

Mr. Bigelow leaned toward him until his angular nose was inches away. "This is your final exam, Charlie. Your final exam. And you've failed, Charlie. As a teacher, you can appreciate how important it is to pass..."

The youth edged nearer, face changing one more time. Charlie Logan knew what the face would become and averted his eyes. The classroom was so cold that his limbs felt frostbitten.

"You failed," murmured Mr. Bigelow.

"A make-up test!" Logan shouted. "Let me take a make-up!"

Mr. Bigelow looked doubtful. "Highly irregular," he said.

"Not in *my* classroom!" Logan screamed. "I give them all the time! Maybe I haven't been such a great teacher, but I always give my students second chances on tests! Fair's fair! Give *me* a make-up!"

Mr. Bigelow considered. The room thawed. "All right, Charlie, a make-up it is!"

Charlie Logan again sat at his own desk. A dream? Had he nodded off? The classroom was empty. Other than his own thudding heart, the only sound was the ticking of the Simplex wall clock. Yes, a dream, plain enough! But what a dream! He wiped wet palms on his pants and shuddered.

"Calm down," he whispered. "Just a crazy, scary dream."

He touched a pencil. Rolled it between his fingers, finding comfort in its mundane reality.

"Just a dream," he whispered again.

But what if it were not a dream?

"It was," he thought. "Had to be."

Are you sure?

"It was a dream," he assured himself. And if it were somehow something more—conscience, perhaps, unearthing long-buried sins—well, okay, all for the best. Guilt was good for the soul. For the rest of his teaching career he would take more interest in his pupils' welfare. Hell, yes! Learn from your mistakes, that would be his motto. Plenty of years ahead to make up for past errors.

He sat back in his chair, stretched (for his neck muscles were yet tight with stress), drew a deep breath, sighed. What a dream! But he had been shocked into a new self-awareness and was displeased with what he beheld. "I'll be a better person after this," he thought. "When I come back here in September..."

But the impact of the dream was abating as the dream faded. Yeah, he might make an effort to be a better person. But it was not too likely. Already he was tired simply contemplating the change.

"Crazy dream," he thought, and stood up. There was a Coke machine in the teachers' lounge, he was thirsty, and summer vacation was so near he could imagine licking sand from some beach bunny's back.

The door opened. "That was your make-up test," said Mr. Bigelow. "A pity you didn't try harder."

Wind hissed through the room. Wind stinking of sulfur.

Behind Mr. Bigelow in the shadows of the hall stood what had been the face-shifting youth. Now, however, the youth had become something huge and hideous and beyond human comprehension. Pale blue flames danced from its pores. It reached for Charlie Logan.

THE EYEGLASSES

When Tommy Johnson visited the thrift shop that Saturday in October, all he was thinking about was Halloween. His junior high always held a costume dance to celebrate the thirty-first. Not that he enjoyed dancing very much. But Amanda Monroe had said she would be there, and Tommy liked her more than he disliked dances.

Trouble was, you could not attend the festivities without a costume. So he had prowled the local Wal-Mart, but all the little kids clogging the Halloween display area had sent him away discouraged. If little kids wanted the costumes, then he didn't. What he needed was something special—something different!

On a whim he had decided to see what Uncle Ned's had to offer. Uncle Ned's, it turned out, had a lot. Everything from outmoded video game systems to Humphrey Bogart-type suits to surgical smocks. Almost every square foot of floor space was crammed with used furniture or clothing or appliances or garishly framed canvases or other assorted bric-a-brac. There was hardly room to squeeze up and down the aisles.

Tommy, who was thirteen, had never before set foot in a thrift shop. True, he had passed this place every day for years on his way to and from school, but until now he had never ventured past its filthy glass doors. Why would he? Thrift shops were where mummified ladies in shapeless dresses frittered away what little remained of their lives. Husky young men who played basketball and hoped to be pro-athletes someday had no business here.

So at first Tommy had felt uncomfortable in Uncle Ned's—but soon he was too busy digging through the racks of second-hand clothes to worry about it. He tried on several double-breasted coats, all so huge that the sleeves hung over his hands and dragged on the linoleum. Hey, all right! He could attach gloves stuffed with newspaper and go as a long-armed ape-like monster. The guys would think it was cool.

But what would Amanda think? "You look ugly! And how can you dance with your hands down there on the ground?"

Better forget that idea. Find something else.

As he meandered to another rack, a khaki safari jacket caught his interest. He examined the fabric. No holes or torn seams. Well, okay. Why not go as an explorer? Sort of like Indiana Jones in those old movies? An action hero. Too cool! Amanda would love this!

At home his father had a wide-brimmed hat that he used for yard work. Dad had bought it on a whim at the San Diego Wild Animal Park, and that hat looked exactly like what Harrison Ford wore in The Temple of Doom. Borrow it (without asking) and the costume would be complete.

A fat lady with fake hair was ahead of him at the solitary checkout counter. Waiting his turn, Tommy poked at a display of combs, broken watches, plastic jewelry, and—what was this?—a glasses case so old that the leather crumbled a bit beneath his touch. Curious, he reached into the case and pulled out the eyeglasses. Not like the kind people wore today. No plastic frames. Wire-rims, with gray round lenses.

"Yes?" The bored cashier at the register was waiting.

"Here." He dumped the safari jacket on the counter. "And this." The eyeglasses were only a dollar. He could afford them too.

Back home and alone, for both his parents were still at work, Tommy searched his father's closet for the hat, then galloped to his own room to conduct a dress rehearsal in front of the bedroom mirror. He was pleased with the way he looked. Even if Indy Jones didn't have them, the gray glasses were a dramatic touch, doubling for vintage sunglasses (Hell, wouldn't a jungle explorer wear 'em?) as well as college professor accessory (Indy taught archaeology, didn't he?). The dance was that very night, and Amanda was sure to go gah-gah over his outfit–and, hopefully, over him.

But the glasses were difficult to see out of. The lenses made the Lakers poster and school sports awards too shadowy. He squinted. The bedroom wall and trophy shelf came into focus. He blinked. The wall and shelf blurred again. Even his jack o' lantern on the bureau seemed lost in shadows.

Vexed, he pulled off the glasses. They had pinched the bridge of his nose. Bending the metal frames, he put them back on. More comfortable. Good.

"Wonder who owned these?" he thought. "They must be real old. Maybe from the time of Indiana Jones, the nineteen-thirties. Cool! Can't get more authentic than that!" No doubt the original owner was long dead and these eyeglasses had been in somebody's trunk until recently.

Well, they looked terrific on, which was the main thing. His costume would be the best at the dance.

How right he was! Other kids pointed, somebody hummed a chorus of the Indiana Jones theme song, and many girls wanted to dance with him.

Amanda, however, never bothered to show up at the school gym where an off-tune local band strummed their electric guitars and shivered the orange-and-black crepe-paper streamers with their vibration. Worse, the eyeglasses aggravated Tommy. He frowned until he invited a headache. As a result, he departed early.

Trick-or-treaters had come and gone.

In the den, his parents were watching television. Tommy stumbled to his room and put on pajamas before troubling to announce his return.

With moonlight casting a pale rectangle of illumination upon the eyeglasses he had left atop the bureau, Tommy fell asleep.

It was of course Halloween night and he was upset by the evening's events, so perhaps a bad dream was inevitable. He tossed in his sleep. Moaned.

In the nightmare, a gray mist oozed through his bedroom window. He tried to call out for his parents but was unable. Terror closed his throat. Terror slammed his heart against his ribs.

The mist churned around him. It became so thick that he could barely see the bureau, the window, or even the walls. Something took shape in the swirling mist. An old man.

Though he knew he must be dreaming, Tommy shuddered in dread. Why he was so afraid he could not have said. The old man was not especially frightening in appearance. Simply wrinkled and stooped, with colorless hair and baggy clothing.

And eyeglasses. Gray round ones, with metal rims.

The same eyeglasses Tommy had purchased at Uncle Ned's.

As he watched, the old man groped his way toward the bed, using a cane. Tap...tap...tap. The cane darted back and forth, probing, guiding. Tap...tap...tap.

"He can't see!" Tommy realized. This fact was more horrifying than the apparition itself.

Tommy woke up screaming.

And went on screaming.

Tommy Johnson was totally blind.

THE WIND

Mrs. Thorne, who lived alone, hated the Santa Ana winds. No season was safe from them. They slithered up when you least expected, rattled windows, shook roofs, pounded metal walls with such force that you feared your mobile home would be uprooted and hurled skyward like some farmhouse from an Oz fantasy.

This morning, as she sipped instant coffee and stared out the patio door at a lone child playing in the street, Mrs. Thorne felt far older than her sixty-two years. Though her hair might be carefully dyed and permed, her figure still slender, her face relatively unwrinkled, none of these assets meant much today. Today her back hurt, her joints were stiff, and a migraine threatened to tear off her head just above the ears. She always felt this way when the Santa Anas stopped by to say hello.

"All in your mind," her husband used to say. "How can wind make you feel lousy?"

It was all in her mind. Psychosomatic nonsense. The headaches, muscle pains. Yes. She readily admitted as much. But these were triggered by fear. And the fear was real. She was afraid of the powerful Santa Anas. Of what they could do.

Now she stood repeating a litany under her breath. "I know nothing bad will happen. No matter how loud the winds get, nothing bad will happen."

From the street the little boy spotted her and waved. She waved back.

"No matter how loud they get, they can't really do anything bad. They can't wreck my home..."

Bad thought! This was a lie, and the woman knew it. Only last week young Mr. Tuttle's spanking-new Suncraft double-wide had lost a driveway awning. Santa Anas had ripped it away and tossed the thing into his miniscule back yard. Three carefully babied lime trees had been pulped. A pink plastic flamingo was no more.

Poor Mr. Tuttle. A nice man too.

Under other circumstances Mrs. Thorne would have loved California. Her husband—with her encouragement, after all!—had chosen to pass his retirement years here. Although all they could afford on his fixed income was a so-called "manufactured house," this mobile home park near Corona was appealing with its landscaped drives, ultra-modern clubhouse, saunas, and even an adjacent golf course. Once settled at Space 112, the Thornes had been ecstatic. No more New Hampshire winters! No more battles with snow that entombed your car during the wee hours of the night, leaving you the fun of disinterring it at daybreak—only to have it buried again three hours later. And, especially, no more chance of Mr. Thorne keeling over from too much sidewalk-shoveling.

No indeed. Mr. Thorne keeled over from too much golfing instead. Death at the seventh green—and he with a par three for that hole!

So here she was, all alone in an aluminum can, her only company a tortoise-shell cat named Snookums. Unless you also counted the little boy still outside braving the gales.

She finished her coffee. Set the cup in the sink.

Snookums strolled across the kitchen table, a trail of white granules in his wake. The sugar bowl!

"Off!"

Snookums turned baleful green eyes upon her.

"Off I said! Right away!"

Snookums screeched and, scattering silverware and breakfast cereal, orbited the room in a frenzy caused not by her rebuke but by a sudden shimmying of the whole house. Gasping, Mrs. Thorne clutched the sink. The mobile home vibrated, swayed, steadied.

Earthquake?

The Santa Anas wailed. "No," they seemed to moan, "only us, only us, only us!"

Still leaning against the sink, Mrs. Thorne waited for her heart to slow. "You're perfectly safe," she told herself fiercely. "Perfectly! Stop being an idiot! These winds can't harm anyone. Why, look out there. See, you old fool? See? That little boy from next door isn't frightened."

She watched the seven-year-old struggle. Flaxen hair whipped into his eyes while his oversized soccer shirt billowed, inflating and deflating with each violent gust, but the child was all smiles as he darted forward, playing out the twine. Five feet behind, a large kite bucked and thrashed.

Mrs. Thorne smiled. This scene calmed her.

Snookums, who had decided to forgive and forget, rubbed against her ankles. Mrs. Thorne glanced down at the cat.

When seconds later she again looked at the street, the little boy was gone.

Wind shrieked.

She thought she heard another shriek too—from far, far away.

ZEROS

The crack extended from one side of the window to the other. Little Jimmy Reynolds, who looked too babyish to be in ninth grade, had hurled his *Warriner's* grammar book against it last week, and the glass–reportedly shatterproof stuff–had cracked.

Mr. Black found himself staring at that window yet again. *Not good!* he thought. *Not good at all! Your job isn't to ponder such defects. The glass wasn't supposed to crack but it did.* ***You're*** *not supposed to crack either, and therefore gaping at that window is definitely a bad idea because it gets you thinking about little Jimmy–and doing* **that** *is ominous, pal–ominous for your peace of mind.*

Mr. Black fought to focus on the task at hand, his ninth grade class. Thirty-four eager faces gazed back at him.

Eager faces...

Eager to learn.

Eager for good grades!

A far cry from the way it used to be, thought Mr. Black, but could not muster a smile. The new methodology motivated students, eliminating bad behavior, rewarding hard work and good study habits–yet, odd as it seemed, he sometimes longed for the old days when discipline problems did arise constantly, when kids ditched class, when fourteen-year-olds complained that Shakespeare was boring, boring, *boring!*

"Mr. Black?" A voice, scarcely audible.

The teacher blinked. "Yes, Melissa?"

Melissa Fairbanks was a frail child whose large brown eyes made her seem like a starving waif in some war-torn ghetto. Right now those same eyes were darting nervously, as if seeking refuge.

"I...uhm...I don't know..."

He looked at her without comprehending. Then he realized it was her turn to answer. They were checking the practice exercises in their Vocabulary Workshop books. While he, their teacher, had been gaping at that crack in the window, tuning them out mentally, they had continued taking their individual turns at answering. Now it was Melissa's turn–and she didn't know the answer.

"Don't be upset," he suggested in his calmest voice. "Take your time."

Panic emanated from the hapless girl. "But I don't know! I just don't know! Mr. Black, I studied this list of words, I studied and studied, but I can't *think, I can't...!*"

He cleared his throat.

The room was silent. Totally, absolutely silent.

"Number twelve," he said, reading from the textbook. "Antonym for 'scrupulous'. Take your time, Melissa. Before you worry about the antonym, ask yourself what the synonym is. What does 'scrupulous' mean?"

Dead silence. Melissa's face was the color of chalk.

"Melissa?" he coaxed.

Melissa buried her face in her hands. She began to sob.

Mr. Black sighed and placed a zero next to the girl's name in his grade book.

"Next?" he said. "Robert? Give me an antonym for 'scrupulous'."

"Immoral," declared Robert.

And so it went, up and down the rows, one youth after another, the answers crisp, enthusiastic, and correct. Only poor Melissa had earned a zero thus far this day–one of *eight* now grafted to her name in his grade book. Eight zeros. *Eight* of them.

Again the cracked window captured his attention. In his mind's eye he envisioned little Jimmy Reynolds hurling the book at the instant he made that tenth error. "I'm sorry, Jimmy, that's the wrong answer," and, **crash,** *Warriner's* shooting through the air, smacking the glass...

And suddenly Mr. Black needed fresh air in the worst way. He gulped and swallowed, sick to his stomach. "Class, study chapter seven in...in *Warriner's* for the next ten minutes. Work alone and be silent." He departed, almost running.

Not too many years ago no teacher could have left his students unattended. Not too many years ago the ninth graders would have torn the room apart if unsupervised...

That was before the advent of the CLINIC philosophy.

Now things were decidedly different. Now there were few if any behavior problems on campus. Now an unsupervised class remained as quiet as the proverbial church mouse.

Mr. Black shoved open the building's side door and stood in the California sunshine. Blue sky overhead, Santa Ana winds banishing all trace of smog; tall green trees; serene, deserted main quad. No loitering students, no discarded soda cans or lunch bags–why, it was Hollywood's conception of the ideal school environment!

The teacher leaned against the English building's cinderblock wall and waited for the nausea to pass. After a long time he opened his eyes.

He waited a little longer, letting the sun bathe him in hot forgetfulness. If he tried, he could almost imagine himself lying on a beach, far from the CLINIC and the kids.

When he returned to class, he made a real effort to avoid seeing the cardboard poster prominently displayed in front of the room. It was mounted next to the wall clock:

> **CAMPUS CLINIC**
> **(Parental Consent is NOT Required, Pursuant to Emergency Educational Reform Act)**
>
> **Referrals: 8:15 A. M. –3:15 P. M. M-F**
>
> **MANDATORY REFERRAL FOR THE FOLLOWING:**
> **A) Misbehavior in Class (Third Offense)**
> **B) Excessive Cutting (Third Offense)**
> **C) Substandard Academic Performance**

Substandard Academic Performance...

Ten zeros in any academic subject equaled substandard performance.

Ten zeros...

Mr. Black hesitated by his lectern. Melissa Fairbanks—he forced his straying thoughts away from her...from her eight zeros ("Two more to go!" screamed a shrill mocking voice in his brain. "Two more, two more!").

Mr. Black moved to his desk—retrieved his copy of *Warriner's.* "All right, class, let's review chapter seven...Exercise Four. Ready?"

They were.

Even Melissa.

Especially Melissa, who now had *eight* zeros.

No one looked at the cracked window, not now, not after Melissa's eighth error earlier today. But it was in their thoughts, that crack—Mr. Black was certain it was!

As was the last glimpse they had all had of little Jimmy Reynolds, shrieking and wildly pitching his textbook mere moments before the red button on Mr. Black's desk had summoned Campus Security. Then little Jimmy had been dragged screaming to the CLINIC.

Substandard performance could not be tolerated.

A collective hush—a holding of breath.

It was again Melissa's turn to answer...

ENTER AT YOUR OWN RISK

...And it was October again, late afternoon sunlight reflecting coldly from the Dutch Colonial's aluminum siding, dead leaves drifting across the overgrown lawn, wind complaining about the sagging porches, the general neglect. Once, many years ago, a Dodge station wagon graced the driveway, a little boy played inside the two-car garage in back of the house, a husband and wife struggled to make ends meet. Now another car stood in the drive, its engine cooling with metronome clicks, and the little boy had come home once more to play in the garage.

Todd Foley brushed his shock of blond hair from his forehead, pocketed the Toyota Corolla keys, and hesitated. Before him—the garage, badly in need of paint. The garage. Waiting.

Until last week he had not been inside that building since 1980. Halloween, 1980, to be specific. Oh, he had lived in the Dutch Colonial with his parents until college. Pratt Institute had freed him from more than a small town environment. For four years, except vacations, he had not been obliged to avert his eyes and pretend the family's garage had ceased to exist.

Enter it?

Play in it?

Hell, he hadn't even been able to look at it for very long at a time without breaking into a cold sweat.

His parents had understood. Even his macho father—especially his father! "You'll get over it," Mike Foley often told his son. "Just takes time." But Mike Foley never got over it, so how could Todd?

Mike Foley...tough, street-wise cop...whose first stroke occurred less than a year after that unspeakable Halloween night when Todd was ten. Mike rallied, recovered completely, returned to work. Suffered a second stroke four years later. Survived. Collected disability.

Died before Todd entered college. Rugged, indestructible Mike Foley, dead before his forty-fifth birthday.

Todd, the only son, winced at this memory. Yes, Mike's life insurance had helped put him through college—those partial scholarships would never have covered the costs of four years at such a top-flight art school—but Todd would gladly have forfeited Pratt altogether in exchange for his father's life.

Now, poised here on the threshold of the clubhouse, Todd steeled himself for what he must face.

Then...

The doors to the garage swung open...

(Not by themselves! Todd thought, *Not under their own power! I opened them, yes, surely!)*

...and Todd Foley, age thirty-five, stepped forward to re-enter the world of Todd Foley, age ten.

"I'm back," he whispered, feeling foolish. But Dr. Munson had urged him to face his fears—and to do this, Todd had decided, required that he re-enact his fantasies and *play the game.*

("We want to play the game," hissed the voices in the dream. "Come play with us; come outside and play," and the little boy shrieked awake, and something had touched his face, caressing, insistent...)

The game.

Todd shivered, despite his leather flight jacket, wool scarf, gloves. All through college he had fought to block out the dreams, the nightmares—had, for the most part, succeeded. Art projects consumed all of his imagination and much of his energy. Lisa demanded the rest. There had been little time to brood about the past. If he dreamed, the dreams seldom rose to the surface of conscious memory.

He had married Lisa a month after graduation, even while still pounding the pavement each day, portfolio under his arm. Neither of them had wanted to wait until he landed his first commercial art job. That same summer a small but promising advertising agency hired him for paste-ups. He and his wife rented an apartment, dingy and overpriced, but they were happy. Her own art training and eventual job helped immensely. With time came better employment, fancier accommodations, occasional trips to Hawaii or Mexico, frequent trips to visit Todd's mother...

(But *never* to visit this garage, Todd, oh no, *never* to venture in here, into *the clubhouse!)*

No nightmares. No midnight horrors. All that was over and done with.

Instead—further joy! A child, a son, born seven years ago. Sean Foley. Strong, muscular little Sean, more like Todd's father than Todd—except for the blond hair.

October wind moaned against the garage doors, making them creak. Todd Foley blinked away the dust that seemed to rise in a cloud from the concrete floor...*(Dust? There can't be any dust! You swept the entire garage Friday!)* ...and edged deeper into the shadowy interior. "I'm back," he said, this time louder. "I'm back, you assholes."

Dr. Munson had instructed Todd to face his fears. So Todd had determined to play the game exactly as he had while a boy.

"Maybe you guys wonder what brings me back after all this time," Todd said, eyes shifting from left to right. He must face each one. Talk to each one. Play the damned game. "See, my Mom died last month. All of a sudden, I was back here trying to sort her stuff and arrange the funeral. Lots of legal things to worry about, too. Gonna sell the house. My wife Lisa was here awhile, but when I saw how long it was gonna take to get things squared away I sent her back home with Sean. 'Course you guys don't know Lisa or Sean, now do you? Guess I never got around to introducing you."

He laughed then. Laughed because *this* was crazy, *he* was crazy for coming up with such a lunatic idea as a *literal* re-creation of his childhood fantasies...

His listeners remained silent. Shadows deepened. Afternoon crept away.

"Anyway, I wouldn't be here in the goddamn garage—pardon me, *clubhouse*—if my bad dreams hadn't started up again. You know, I figured I'd beaten that problem way back when. Guess not.

Dr. Munson thinks my mother's death triggered the nightmares. That, and my living here at the house these past few weeks. In case you wondered, Mom's death was awful for me...awful..."

The listeners said nothing. Todd glared at them. They glared back, a multitude of frozen grimaces, rigid postures, papier-mâché claws. "Bastards," Todd muttered. "Bastards! You don't scare me. Try to move! One of you—any of you—try! I dare you. Let's play the goddamn *game!* Like when I was a kid. The *game!* You remember."

The listeners made no movement. Leaves rustled outside. Otherwise, silence.

"Don't feel like going for a stroll?" Todd asked. "Okay, how about *saying* something? Anybody feel chatty?"

But no one did. How could they? These wretched dummies were composed of coat hanger wire, newspaper, old clothes, papier-mâché. Though their visages resembled various creatures from classic horror films, they were not alive—were not even actors disguised to frighten. In some cases the paste and paper visages were not yet dry, for Todd had worked for only three days to finish all thirteen of them—Wednesday, Thursday, yesterday. Countless hours, a race against the calendar, for Dr. Munson had inadvertently inspired this try at self-regulated therapy at Tuesday's session, which meant that the deadline was today, Halloween.

The anniversary of that night long gone...

"Todd, you must confront your fears," Munson had said. "Otherwise you will never banish them. But if you face them, examine them fully, you'll discover that whatever happened involving those make-believe monsters of yours happened only in your mind. Imagination..."

"But I wasn't the only one who saw them come to life. They *killed* Richard Buckman!"

"The fifth grade bully? Your nemesis? He fell off a bridge."

"They *threw* him off!"

"That's not what the old newspaper accounts say."

"I *saw* them do it!"

"Were you there with them when it happened?"

"No. But I saw it happen in my dreams. And the next day Richard was dead."

"Are you sure that's the order of events, Todd? Are you sure? Or did you perhaps hear about Richard's death and *later* dream that your monsters had murdered him?"

"No. No! I dreamed the events right while they were happening."

"Did you, Todd? How can you be so positive? You were only ten. That was a long while ago. Nobody's memory is perfect. The more your age distances you from occurrences, the less accurate your recollections. And your parents *never* discussed with you what happened, you said. They chose to pretend *nothing* had happened. Perhaps, in truth, nothing did, except in your imagination."

More and more Todd found himself wondering if Munson were right. So much of that period in his childhood Todd had managed to blank out. Traumatic response to nerve-shattering episode? Or the gradual forgetting of mere nightmares? He could not be certain.

"You'll get over it," his father had said. But over what? Something straight out of hell, so monstrous that the aftereffects sent a strong cop to an early grave? Or a childhood bout with mental illness?

There had been the *clubhouse*. That much he recalled. Half the garage had been his, a place to play, and he had created numerous dummies over many weeks and had placed them in old chairs or propped them against the walls. His "friends". Dracula, Frankenstein, the Wolfman, the Mummy, a ghoul, all the rest—oh yes, he remembered that, his obsession with monster movies, his clubhouse (actually his *monster museum)*—and *the game*.

The game. Nothing more than pretending. The figures in the garage became his imaginary pals. He talked to them, shared adventures with them, chased away the loneliness a shy child often experiences.

But *the game* grew more intense day by day. Todd began to have trouble separating fantasy from reality.

Hadn't the figures gained a life of their own, somehow siphoning energy from him? Hadn't they butchered Richard Buckman, a kid in Todd's school, a punk who terrorized Todd and the other fifth graders?

He frowned as he considered these things. The past blurred, got jumbled and muddy. Hadn't Todd's father finally burned the dummies? That must have actually happened because the garage had been without Todd's figures for almost a quarter of a century now.

And yet...and yet...what else? There was more, surely! Dreadful blinks of memory, things best left unremembered: pumpkins, jack o' lanterns (Halloween eve!)...voices calling, summoning him...something about graves...the rural cemetery...

"No!" He gasped the word aloud. "No!" He could not deal with it, would not! Shut it out as always! Slam the door!

In the last few minutes the garage had grown darker. Night was close at hand. Todd focused his attention on the present moment—and the now hard-to-see dummies seated in the old chairs or lurking in corners. "Face your fears," Munson had advised. Doubtless the good doctor had never guessed exactly how Todd would do this. Years of psychiatric bills were not Todd's idea of a confrontation with his past. Hardly.

Munson would have been appalled. Todd knew this and could not have cared less.

Re-create the monsters. Play the game. Talk to 'em! Pretend they're alive! And do this on Halloween night, the anniversary of whatever had taken place in 1980! A *literal* showdown with the past...

Todd sensed that this was his only chance to prove to himself that all the half-forgotten nightmares from his youth were nothing more than that, nightmares.

"Getting dark," he murmured conversationally. "Your kind of night, guys. Overcast, not a star in the sky."

The figures, mere lumps of shadow, seemed more real in this deepening gloom. Was that a sigh? An in-drawn breath? No, absurd! He attempted to make out individual faces. Impossible.

"Better let you in on a secret, too. It's October thirty-first. How about that? Talk about special nights! This is when all evil is loosed on the world. At least, so tradition says. You believe in tradition?"

Absolute silence.

He waited.

The silence seemed palpable.

"Somebody want to say something?"

Obviously not.

A long time he waited. And the quiet and the situation started to unnerve him.

At last, way off in the distance, a sound. Faint laughter.

Todd's heart lurched at the noise. Instinctively he cringed. The laughter became louder. But it did not originate in the garage.

Kids! Out on the street! Trick-or-treaters!

A rush of relief and Todd too was laughing. Turning toward the garage entrance, he wondered if those kids would visit the Dutch Colonial.

AND–

THE GARAGE DOORS SLAMMED SHUT...

AND–

DESPITE THE INSTANTANEOUS BLACKNESS TODD COULD ***SEE*** *HIS DUMMIES VIVIDLY BECAUSE GREEN GLOBULES OF LIGHT CRAWLED LIKE ALIEN INSECTS UP AND DOWN EACH FIGURE.*

THEN ONE OF THE DUMMIES ROSE FROM ITS CHAIR.

"NO!" TODD CRIED.

THE DUMMY SWAYED, JERKED, DID A PALSIED DANCE–AND EXPLODED. COAT HANGER WIRE USED AS ITS SKELETAL FRAMEWORK ROCKETED FORWARD.

TODD SCREAMED.

THE WIRE PLUNGED DEEP INTO HIS SHOULDER AND UPRAISED FOREARM.

AND THE OTHER DUMMIES EXPLODED, ONE AFTER ANOTHER, AND THE GARAGE VIBRATED WITH THE IMPACT OF A THOUSAND FLYING FRAGMENTS. THE GARAGE DOORS BURST OPEN. TODD HALF-FELL, HALF-LUNGED INTO THE YARD.

Children were there, curious and noisy. Todd writhed to his knees, gasping, arrows of metal protruding from shoulder, arm...nowhere else. Lethal wire shafts blasted in every direction, and he with no additional wounds...

They're saving me for something else, he thought. *A game...*

("LET'S PLAY ***THE GAME,****"* whispered a voice in the wind. *"READY, TODD?")*

Twenty or more costumed children crowded nearer: witches, skeletons, ghosts, two look-alike Donald Ducks. Trick-or-treat bags no longer held much interest. A few adults also ran into the yard.

Questions were shouted, individual words lost in the excitement of that frantic moment.

Todd staggered to his feet. Tattered bits of cloth lay everywhere...chunks of papier-mâché...twisted wire...splinters of chairs...

No dummies. None left. Was it over? Was that all?

"You're bleeding!" shrieked one of the Donald Ducks.

Todd glanced down. A thin string of red liquid flowed down his flight jacket. As he watched, drops spilled to the ground.

AS IF THAT WAS THE NECESSARY CATALYST, GREEN LIGHT CRACKLED FROM THE DEBRIS SCATTERED THROUGHOUT THE GARAGE. IN AN INSTANT BITS OF WIRE AND FRAGMENTS OF PAPIER-MÂCHÉ WERE AIRBORNE. THEY SWARMED INTO THE HALLOWEEN SKY LIKE INSANE HORNETS. PEOPLE GAPED, TOO LATE TOOK TO THEIR HEELS.

THREE CHILDREN DIED AS WIRES RIPPED THROUGH THEIR BODIES ONLY TO RISE INTO THE AIR AND RIP THROUGH AGAIN.

DONALD DUCK ONE AND DONALD DUCK TWO WERE ENSNARED BY A CLOUD OF DEBRIS, CARRIED A HUNDRED FEET INTO THE HEAVENS, AND DROPPED.

TWO OF THE ADULTS STRANGLED. PAPIER-MÂCHÉ FORCED ITS WAY DOWN THEIR THROATS.

"NO!" TODD SCREAMED OVER AND OVER. "NO! NO! ***NO!"***

AND-

MORE EXPLOSIONS, AS ALL THE DARTING, FLYING SCRAPS DISINTEGRATED, BECOMING IN AN INSTANT A MILLION GREEN PARTICLES OF LIGHT...

PARTICLES THAT ENGULFED ONE FLEEING BYSTANDER AFTER ANOTHER, AND–

("Ready to go to the school Halloween party?" Lisa, some seventy-nine miles away and impatient, asked her son Sean Foley.

"In a minute," the child shouted. "Can't get my shoe tied.")

–AND–TODD STAGGERED TOWARD HIS CAR

PARKED THERE IN THE DRIVEWAY, WHILE BEHIND HIM PEOPLE SCREAMED AND DIED.

"LIKE ACID!" TODD GASPED, NOT EVEN AWARE HE SPOKE. "LIKE ACID!"

(ACID. FLYING CLOUDS OF GHASTLY GREEN FLUORESCENCE THAT SWEPT OVER ONE INDIVIDUAL AFTER ANOTHER, DISSOLVING AWAY FLESH INSTANTANEOUSLY, LEAVING TATTERED CLOTHES, DESICCATED SKIN, CHALK-WHITE BONES...)

THE CAR! HE STUMBLED, RIGHTED HIMSELF, REACHED FOR THE DOOR HANDLE. PAIN RADIATED FROM HIS ARM, HIS SHOULDER, BUT HE MANAGED TO PULL HIMSELF INTO THE DRIVER'S SEAT–MANAGED TO SLAM THE DOOR, LOCK IT, START THE ENGINE.

("TODD," WAILED A VOICE IN THE WIND, "TODD, DON'T GO! THE FUN HASN'T EVEN STARTED YET! PLAY THE GAME WITH US!")

*AND, KNOWING HE MUST NOT, TODD PULLED HIS GAZE FROM THE SIDE-VIEW MIRROR EVEN AS HE SLAMMED THE TOYOTA INTO REVERSE AND SHOT UP THE DRIVE, AWAY FROM THE **CLUBHOUSE**...*

*CARNAGE EVERYWHERE! WITHERED, SHRIVELED BODIES (**SKELETONS!**) WHO HAD LIVED AND BREATHED BUT BRIEF MOMENTS BEFORE!*

(AGAIN, THE VOICE: "TIME TO PLAY SOME MORE!")

*(SIMULTANEOUSLY TWO THINGS HAPPENED: TODD LOST CONTROL OF HIS VEHICLE, SMASHING INTO THE SIDE OF HIS PARENTS' HOUSE–**AND**...)*

PULSING BUGS OF GREEN LIGHT SWAM OVER THE SKELETONS. THESE BUGS SKITTERED FASTER, FASTER, UNTIL A TRANSPARENT SLIME OF ILLUMINATION ENCASED THE BONES. A RIPPLE OF MOTION FROM ONE OF THE DEAD...

TODD STARED THROUGH THE WINDSHIELD. "COME OUT AND PLAY!" SOMETHING CALLED. THEN THEY WERE UPON THE CAR, TWENTY OR MORE OF THEM, THEIR BLACK EYE SOCKETS SEEKING, THEIR

SKULL FACES PRESSED AGAINST THE WINDOWS...

METAL GAVE WAY.

GLASS SHATTERED.

THEY SPRANG INSIDE THE AUTOMOBILE.

"GAME'S OVER!" HISSED THE WIND.

AND–

Todd Foley was rigid, eyes locked on the dummy nearest him. Night had enveloped the garage. The figures in their chairs seemed but amorphous lumps, featureless, unrecognizable. But a hint of green light peeked from the closest figure's eyes–peeked and hid.

Todd managed a few deep breaths. Wiped his forehead. Licked his lips.

What had happened? Had he somehow dozed off a few seconds?

Yes. That was it. Of course!

Unless...

"Game's over!"

Were *they* demonstrating what *they* could do if he challenged *them*? A possible scenario, presented for his entertainment and edification?

Todd zippered his leather jacket against the fierce cold. Tried to smile. Failed.

Without looking back, he hurried to his car, climbed in, and very, *very* carefully backed up the driveway and into the street.

(Seventy-nine miles away, in New York City, Sean Foley slipped the Frankenstein mask over his head and inspected the results in a bedroom mirror. For a seven-year-old he made an impressive monster indeed.

"We're going to be late if you don't get a move on," his mother announced from the living room.

"Be right there," Sean yelled, tone muffled by the false face. He grabbed rubber hands from the bureau, horrible deformed claw-like things that he would wear like gloves...

And, from his closet, a faint draft stirred dust motes. The door shuddered open an inch. Dull green light flickered from within.

"Come play with us!" whispered a voice.)